FOREIGN EXCHANGE

After disembarking in Salonika, Frank walked over and tugged at Joe's arm. "Don't be too obvious about it," he said quietly, "but take a look at the big car by the gangplank. See anyone familiar?"

Joe turned casually and recognized one drab figure moving through the crowd of brightly dressed tourists.

His code name was the Gray Man, and he worked for a super-secret government organization known only as the Network. He was a heavy hitter in the game of international intrigue.

"What's *he* doing here?" Joe wanted to know. "And what was he doing on our ship?"

Frank turned to his brother. "One thing's for sure," he said. "If there's any connection between the Network's business and us, we're involved in something a lot more dangerous than a student tour."

Books in THE HARDY BOYS CASEFILES® Series

Available from ARCHWAY Paperbacks

THE HARDY BOYS CASEFILES NO. 25

THE BORDERLINE CASE

FRANKLIN W. DIXON

AN ARCHWAY PAPERBACK
Published by POCKET BOOKS
New York   London   Toronto   Sydney   Tokyo   Singapore

AN ARCHWAY PAPERBACK *Original*

An Archway Paperback published by
POCKET BOOKS, a division of Simon & Schuster Inc.
1230 Avenue of the Americas, New York, NY 10020

Copyright © 1989 by Simon & Schuster Inc.
Cover art copyright © 1989 Brian Kotzky
Produced by Mega-Books of New York, Inc.

ISBN: 0-671-72452-5

First Archway Paperback printing March 1989

10 9 8 7 6 5 4 3 2

THE HARDY BOYS, AN ARCHWAY PAPERBACK and colophon are registered trademarks of Simon & Schuster Inc.

THE HARDY BOYS CASEFILES is a trademark of Simon & Schuster Inc.

Printed in the U.S.A.

IL 7+

THE BORDERLINE CASE

Chapter

1

"WHAT IS THIS STUFF, ANYWAY?"

Joe Hardy held up a fork holding something he'd speared from his lunch plate.

His older brother, Frank, glanced up at the fork. "I believe it's squid, Joe."

Joe dropped the fork as if it were red-hot and stared down in mock horror.

"*Squid?* You serious, or just trying to gross me out?"

Frank leaned forward. "If you look closely, you'll see the little suckers on the tentacles—"

Joe continued to stare. "I *knew* I shouldn't have ordered anything I couldn't pronounce." Joe was talking about the food in Greece on his summer student exchange trip. He shoved the plate away.

"Lighten up," Frank replied. "Hamburgers and pizza will still be at home when we get there. You might give Greece and its food a chance before you put it down."

Sitting next to Joe was the Hardys' friend Chet Morton. He looked up from his plate long enough to observe, "You know, it really isn't bad. And this pink stuff is great on bread."

Frank laughed. "Chet never met a meal he didn't like."

The Hardys were part of a group of Bayport students sitting around a big table at an outdoor restaurant in Piraeus, the port of Athens. It was their first day in Greece. Later that afternoon they would board a ship to Salonika, Greece's second-largest city. Salonika was in the north, only forty miles from the border of Yugoslavia.

The exchange students included another good friend of Frank and Joe's, Phil Cohen, and a boy of Greek heritage, Peter Stamos, who spoke up then.

"That 'pink stuff' is called taramosalata, and it's made from fish eggs and oil—"

"Peter, please," Joe cut in. "There're some things it's better not to know."

The chaperon of the Bayport group was a fussy-looking man with glasses—a Professor

Morton Prynne. He had been frowning at Joe from his place at the head of the table. "One purpose of student exchange is to learn about the customs and habits of other lands. It wouldn't hurt you to try the food."

Joe muttered under his breath.

"Come on, Joe," Frank urged. "Don't you remember Dad telling us about eating camel hump in North Africa and rattlesnake in Arizona?"

Their father, Fenton Hardy, was an internationally known private eye. His work took him to all parts of the world.

Morton Prynne cleaned his glasses, then tapped the table with a spoon. "May I have your attention for a moment? As long as we have time before we board our ship, we might go over our schedule for the next few days."

"Bor-r-r-ing," Chet said through clenched teeth.

"After lunch we will go directly to the pier, where we will go aboard. The luggage is already loaded. We leave the harbor at three this afternoon, and reach Salonika at two P.M. tomorrow. You will be sleeping two to a cabin. You should already have your room assignments. If anyone has misplaced his or hers, please see me after lunch.

"We will be met in Salonika by Mr. Spiros Stamos, who will lead a Greek contingent of students to America. I remind you that Spiros Stamos is the uncle of our own Peter Stamos. They have never met, and in honor of that meeting, and to celebrate our arrival, there will be a party tomorrow night, hosted by Mr. Stamos and his son and daughter.

"For the next two days, Mr. Stamos will be our guide for the many interesting sights in Salonika and the area."

Joe Hardy stifled a groan. "Ruins," he stated darkly. "Ruins and more ruins—we'll be climbing over piles of old rocks."

Prynne interrupted Joe's gloomy prediction. "Please remember—especially you, Joe—that you represent American youth. Whatever Mr. Stamos may have planned for this visit, I expect that you will behave in a way that will reflect positively on our country. You will treat Mr. Stamos with more respect than you have given me."

Phil Cohen grinned. "In other words," he whispered, "shut up and eat your squid."

Opposite Prynne sat a Greek school teacher named Nicholas Kaliotis, serving as the professor's assistant and, when necessary, as an interpreter. He looked up, his broad grin taking some of the sting out of Prynne's stuffy speech.

"I'm told that we'll be visiting one of the many excellent beaches near the city." He smiled. "We Greeks want you to know that we have more than monuments and ruins. I might even be able to find some American-style hamburgers in Salonika."

As Kaliotis had hoped, the mood of the group brightened.

Chet tapped Joe on the shoulder. "If you don't plan to eat any of that," he pointed to Joe's untouched lunch, "do you mind if I take some of that . . . whatever the pink stuff is called?"

Joe slid the plate over. "Here you go, big guy. I'll stick to bread and water for now."

"Right," Frank said, "you go ahead and soak up some Greek culture, Chet."

Phil Cohen turned to Peter Stamos. "You've never met any of your relatives in Salonika? At all?"

Peter shook his head. "My father went to Greece for visits once or twice. But I've never been to Greece before."

"Do you speak any Greek?" asked Frank.

"I speak some, and I understand a little more. My folks didn't use it around the house—except when they didn't want us to understand what they were saying."

"Hey, Peter," said Joe. "Maybe you can help us out while we're on the boat with some basic vocabulary. I'm still having trouble with 'please' and 'thank you.' "

"Sure. I guarantee that by the time we reach Salonika, you'll be saying 'please' and 'thank you' just like a native. Maybe even—"

"Hey! Americans!"

The raspy shout cut off all conversation. On the sidewalk, behind a low white-metal fence, three scruffy men glared at the group. They wore old and dirty denim pants, and two had dark blue peacoats. The third wore a shabby sweater. All three looked as if they hadn't shaved or showered in the past few days. All three looked like sailors.

"What are you doing here, Americans?" the guy in the sweater snarled in heavily accented English. "Nobody want you in Greece! Why you don't go home?"

A second one joined in. "Go away, Yankee pigs. Greek people sick of you!"

Prynne leaned in toward the students. "Pay no attention. It seems they've been drinking. If you ignore them, they'll leave, but if you answer, it will only get worse."

"Hey, talk to me, Americans!" The first taunter leaned over the fence. "You think you too good to talk to me?" He spat on the ground near the table—right by Joe's foot.

Joe sat still, but his face flushed under his blond hair.

"Hey, pretty boy, what's the matter? You don't like Greeks now, pretty boy?"

The ringleader had an ugly grin on his skinny, pockmarked face.

"Joe—" Frank warned, his dark eyes flashing.

But Joe just held up his fork. "Greeks, yes," he said. "You, no."

Nicholas Kaliotis jumped up, shouting something in Greek, and the three toughs vaulted the low fence. A waiter rushed to intercept them but was knocked flat by one of the three with a disdainful backhanded swipe.

Suddenly there were large, ugly knives gleaming in the thugs' hands. They stalked toward the Americans, murder in their eyes.

Chapter

2

Joe leaped to his feet as one of the men came for him. The thug stopped a few feet from Joe, sizing him up, staying in a half-crouch and occasionally feinting. His knife hand lazily moved from side to side, making short jabs toward his target. Then he stepped forward quickly, with his knife aimed at Joe's stomach.

Chet Morton, sitting unnoticed, had quietly picked up a Coke bottle. Now, moving with a speed and agility unexpected of someone his size and weight, he brought it down with a chopping blow on the wrist of the man's knife hand. The weapon clattered to the ground as the attacker grunted in pain, cradling his injured wrist in his other hand.

Wasting no time, Joe caught his enemy on the jaw with a right that had all his weight and strength behind it. The man hit the pavement like a sack of cement and lay motionless.

Meanwhile, a second assailant was going for Prynne. He circled the students, then zeroed in on the head of the table, his knife in front of him, edge up, as experienced blade-fighters keep theirs. Prynne scrambled out of his chair and backed up one step, staying just beyond range of the sharp point and looking terrified. His attacker grinned—this little fellow in the eyeglasses seemed like an easy mark.

But as the attacker started his lunge, Prynne snatched a cup of hot tea from the table and flung the steaming contents into the thug's face. Screaming, knife and attack forgotten, the man went down, clutching his scalded face.

The last of the attackers, the ringleader, had hung back. Now, seeing how things had gone, he spun away, cleared the fence in one bound, and took off running down the street. Frank sprang up, intending to chase him down.

Prynne called out as Frank started to move: "Frank! No!"

Frank wheeled and looked at Prynne in surprise. "Why not, Mr. Prynne? These guys should get arrested. I can have that one back here in—"

"Frank, that'll do! Just leave things alone,"

snapped Prynne. Then he softened slightly, explaining, "You haven't spent time in Greece, Frank. You can't imagine the amount of red tape we'd get tangled up in with the police. We might be stuck here for hours, even days. We'd miss our ship, wreck our schedule. The entire tour would be ruined, and all over a foolish business with a few men who had a few drinks too many. Best not to get involved."

Rubbing his bruised knuckles, Joe said, "What about the two guys lying here? Are we going to let them go, too? Maybe we owe them an apology for being so hostile—I mean, all they did was try to stick us with those Greek toothpicks!"

Prynne glowered at Joe. "Certainly we won't let them go. I'll just have a word with the manager here and see to it that they're turned over to the authorities. In the meantime we can be on our way to the pier. Justice will be served, and we won't have to be involved."

With that he signaled to the manager and drew him aside. As they talked, Joe tapped Chet on the shoulder.

"Hey, thanks for the help. I owe you one."

Chet blushed and smiled. "I already owe *you* a few, remember?"

Prynne paid for lunch, and for the damage done by the attackers. Then the manager shook hands and called out two waiters and a busboy to take charge of the thugs. Meanwhile, Prynne hurriedly got his students to their feet and shepherded them off the terrace and toward the pier.

Half an hour later the American students stood at the pier at the end of a long line of passengers. The procession moved very slowly—each would-be boarder went through a rigorous examination before being allowed to proceed.

Joe watched the lack of progress with growing impatience. "I don't see what all the rush was for back at the restaurant," he complained. "We could have spent the whole afternoon clearing that mess up with the police and still have been in plenty of time for this."

Frank sighed and ran his fingers through his brown hair. "Well, Prynne's right about one thing," he said. "We've never been to Greece, and he has. Maybe he's right about dealing with the local law. Let's just take it easy and assume he knows what he's doing."

"Okay." But Joe still wasn't very happy. "It just feels weird, ducking out like that after being attacked, almost as if we were the criminals. I bet Dad wouldn't be too crazy about it either."

Frank thought for a moment. "Maybe so," he said. "But we're here and he's not." Then he spotted Peter Stamos and waved him over.

"Hi, Frank, Joe! Too bad we can't fight our way through. That's some right you've got there, Joe. You put that ugly customer out with one punch!"

Joe smiled and said, "Thanks to Chet and his trusty Coke bottle."

"Peter," asked Frank, "you remember just before those guys came at us, Mr. Kaliotis jumped up and yelled something at them?"

Peter replied, "Yeah. What about it?"

Frank continued, "Did you understand what he said? Was your Greek good enough to follow it?"

Peter's forehead wrinkled in concentration as he thought back. Then he shook his head, saying, "I didn't really catch it, Frank. I mean, everything happened so fast. He was yelling something like 'These are important Americans, so don't mess with them . . .' Some kind of warning." He shrugged. "Why do you ask?"

"Oh, no special reason, I was just wondering," Frank said. "Hey, what do you know! This line actually seems to be moving. I was beginning to think we'd have to camp here for the night."

The American kids began to pull out their passports and tickets. They passed the check-in booth and started up the passenger ramp. At the top of the ramp, Frank turned back for a final look at Piraeus.

The pier was bordered by a busy waterfront street with a scattering of sailors' bars, shops, and a steady stream of traffic. At the corner nearest the pier, a man with a knit cap and jeans stood leaning against a wall. He had a thin ferret face and needed a shave badly. His eyes never left the group of Americans. The man walked over to a parked car and leaned in through a window to talk.

Then the car's passenger door opened, and two men got out. They were similarly dressed, in heavy wool coats, jeans, and knit caps.

As Frank turned away to step onto the boat, the three men joined the boarding line.

All through the afternoon and early evening, the ship sailed in relatively calm water between islands. But after dinner it reached the open sea and began to pitch and roll.

For the students from Bayport, the unfamiliar food and the constant swaying had a nasty effect on their stomachs. By nine in the evening, most of the group had retreated to their cabins, trying to find some comfort in bed.

Joe Hardy was one of the sickest of all. When Frank suggested a walk on the deck, Joe only groaned and turned his slightly green and sweaty face away. "Walking? Even talking is too much for me." So Frank went to search out other company.

But the only other young person who wasn't laid low for the night was Chet Morton, who happily agreed to take a little fresh air on deck. The two went out and leaned against the rail on their deck, looking out over the sea.

The moon laid down a white path for the ship to follow as it cut through the whitecaps. Frank thought that he could make out the shoreline in the distance, a thin smudge slightly darker than sea or sky.

Frank grinned at Chet. "We must be the only ones who have their sea legs."

"Yeah, I guess so," agreed Chet, who liked the notion that he was a better sailor than the others. He sucked in his belly and squinted out to sea, thinking of himself as an old salt. A few minutes passed in friendly silence.

"Say, Frank," Chet said at length, "this sea air is giving me an appetite. You think they have a snack bar anywhere on this boat? A hot fudge sundae would really be—"

"I don't think you'll find anything open this late," replied Frank with a grin. "Besides, even if they did have late-night service, it'd most likely be squid or octopus or fish eggs."

"I'd settle for that," Chet sighed.

Frank smiled. "Tough it out then. You'll have to wait until morning."

Suddenly a loud thump echoed from a nearby passageway. A harsh, whispering voice followed, too faint for the boys to make out the words.

Chet turned to Frank. "What was—?" Frank cut him off with a quick "Shhh."

He stood and listened intently and then looked around. The whispers changed to scraping sounds and seemed to be getting closer. Motioning for Chet to follow, Frank moved noiselessly to a point where they would be hidden in deep shadow. They pressed themselves against a bulkhead and waited.

Three figures shuffled onto the deck, visible only as darker shapes in the dim light. Frank saw two guys half dragging a third between them. As they neared the rail, the moonlight hit them.

With a jolt, Frank recognized the figure being pulled along as Morton Prynne!

Chapter

3

PRYNNE LOOKED HALF-CONSCIOUS. Frank and
Chet exchanged a quick glance, and then
charged forward from their shadowy hiding
place.

The boys had the element of surprise on their
side. Reaching the closer of the two, Frank
grabbed him by the shoulder and yanked him
around, breaking the guy's grip on Prynne. He
stiff-armed the man in the midsection. His
breath came out in one loud *whoosh* before he
fell to his hands and knees.

Chet had taken the other one by the collar
and belt and lifted him the way a pro wrestler
might. He then bounced him off the bulkhead.
The man hit with a metallic *clunk* and slid to

the floor, where a weak side-to-side movement of his head showed that he was still breathing. He was probably trying to figure out what had hit him.

With both of the mystery men out of action, Frank turned to Prynne. From somewhere just beyond his line of sight a heavy body threw itself at him. Frank, caught completely off guard, was propelled toward the rail by the momentum of the surprise attack.

He slammed into the wooden railing and stopped, momentarily stunned. He felt himself being lifted then, and had a brief flash of churning water below him and of a distant, barely visible shoreline. There seemed to be no way of stopping whoever it was from sending him for a deadly moonlight swim.

And then, just as unexpectedly as the surprise attack had begun, Frank's still unknown enemy lost his grip, dropping Frank heavily onto the deck. Frank struck his head sharply against the rail on the way down. Stunned and breathless, he was only vaguely conscious that someone had come to his rescue. After a brief pause to recover his wits and his wind, he struggled to his knees.

He stayed that way until he was sure that no bones had been broken, and then, gritting his teeth, staggered painfully to his feet.

He saw Chet, leaning against the bulkhead

17

holding his head, and Prynne, who was now up on one elbow.

There was no one else around. The unknown men had vanished, leaving the three Americans, bruised but breathing, alone on the rolling deck.

Frank went to help Prynne get up as Chet slowly joined them.

"Thank you, boys," said Prynne faintly. "I feel all right now, I . . ." He swayed, and clutched at Frank's shoulder for support.

"Sir," said Frank, "I think you may need medical attention. You could have a concussion or internal injuries. Why don't I stay with you while Chet looks for the authorities."

Even though he was battered, Prynne hadn't lost his pride. "Don't be ridiculous!" he snapped, straightening his clothes and glaring at Frank. "I'm in no need of anything, except the opportunity to go back to my cabin to lie down."

Frank looked narrowly at the man's pale face. "Look, Mr. Prynne, someone has to let the ship's captain know what just happened. Even if you won't see a doctor, we can't just—"

"I have only one need right now," Prynne said, cutting him off. "And that is to get back to my bunk and rest. If you want to help me, you can help me there."

Frank and Chet looked helplessly at each

other as their teacher tottered into the passage-way.

Chet stared after him. "What do you think we should do?" he asked.

Frank didn't speak at first. Then he shook his head. "I think if we follow him, we'll probably get our heads bitten off. Maybe we'd better do what he says. Let's turn in for the night and take care of business in the morning."

But Chet was still curious. "Do you figure those two guys really wanted to dump the professor over the side?"

"It looked that way from where *I* was standing." Frank gave Chet a puzzled look. "*Two* guys? Didn't you see the third guy?"

Chet stared. "What third guy? All I saw was the two we went after, the ones with Prynne. There was another?"

"There had to be," answered Frank. "After I took care of the one I grabbed, someone jumped me from behind and tried to dump me overboard. There didn't seem to be a thing I could do about it. Then someone took the new guy off me. I thought maybe it was you."

"Don't look at me," protested Chet. "I thought my man was down and out, but he tripped me up somehow, and I think he kicked me in the head before he took off. By the time

I came to again, there were just the three of us."

Frank was at a loss. Who could have saved him? He walked over to the rail and looked out at the sea, trying to put it all together.

Chet joined him. "There was something else kind of funny, Frank. I can't be sure of it, but—"

"What?" Frank turned to his friend.

Chet shrugged. "Everything was pretty mixed up and dark, but I thought the guy who attacked me was one of those guys from the restaurant this afternoon."

The Hardys got up at noon the next day to find the sun shining, the winds calm, and the sea smooth. Joe stretched and yawned, sitting up in his bunk while Frank did pushups, all the exercise their cramped cabin allowed.

Interrupting a pushup, Frank lifted his head to glance at his brother. "Looks like you're back among the living today," he observed.

Joe swung his legs out of the bunk and sat up, smiling. "It's amazing," he said. "Today I feel great and ready to eat about ten pounds of steak. Last night if someone had asked me to choose between food and being tossed over the side of the ship, I'd have had to flip a coin."

Frank got to his feet. "Funny you should

mention going over the side," he said. He told Joe about the events of the evening before.

Joe's smile faded as he listened. "Sounds like a pretty close call," he said.

Frank shrugged.

"I should have been there for you," Joe growled.

"Hey, go easy on yourself," said Frank. "When you're sick, you're sick. Anyway, Chet did a pretty good job standing in for you."

"I don't like this," Joe insisted with a frown. "Something's not right. Let's find the captain and let him know—"

"Whoa, take it easy." Frank raised his hands. "I think it'd be better if we talk to Prynne first. Whoever attacked him has nowhere to go—they're still somewhere aboard."

Joe jumped to his feet. "Then let's get cleaned up, find Prynne, and talk to him—after we find something to eat."

Frank grinned as he pulled on a pair of jeans. "Trust you to get your priorities straight."

A few minutes later they entered a small snack bar on an upper deck. Phil Cohen and Chet Morton were sitting at a table, and Phil waved the Hardys over.

"Chet told me about the fun and games last night," said Phil as the Hardys sat. "You okay, Frank?"

"I've got some bruises where I hit the rail."

21

Frank rubbed his ribs. "No big deal—it could have been worse. How are *you* feeling?"

Phil smiled weakly. "Now that my stomach is back where it belongs, I'm fine. Last night it kept trying to crawl out through my throat."

Joe said, "I think some plain breakfast food will help keep mine in place. What's safe to eat here?"

Chet looked up from his plate. "Try some of these cakes, Joe. This one's my favorite. It's filled with chopped nuts and cinnamon, and the honey is the best I've ever tasted. And they have this soda, it's a kind of sour cherry flavor, I think it's called, uh, veeseenada, or something, and—"

"Easy, big fella," said Phil, laughing. "Don't strip your gears." Then he turned to Frank and Joe. "You'd probably like this spinach pie," he said. "And the cakes are good, if you have a serious sweet tooth, like our pal here."

They signaled to a waiter, who took the Hardys' order. Before he could leave, Chet stopped him. "Um, as long as you're here, bring a couple more of those spinach pies. Oh, and a couple of the ones filled with custard."

The waiter gaped at him, not certain he'd heard correctly. "You want two more of this *and* two more of this one here? Yes?"

"And another one of these veeseenadas to wash it down," finished Chet happily.

Chet noticed the others grinning at him, and shrugged. "It's the sea air," he said.

"Yeah, right," said Joe.

"Take it easy on Chet," Frank cut in. "He had a busy time last night.

"Speaking of last night," Frank continued in a more serious vein, "maybe it'd be better if we kept all of that to ourselves for a while. At least until we've talked to Prynne anyway."

Chet and Phil agreed to keep quiet.

"Have you seen Prynne yet today?" asked Frank.

"Nope," answered Phil. "We got up late and came right in here."

From outside came a babble of cheers and excited voices. Nicholas Kaliotis stopped in the entrance and saw the students.

"Better eat fast, friends, we've arrived! We are coming into the port of Salonika!"

An hour later the ship had docked, and the group was waiting on deck to disembark. There was still no sign of Morton Prynne.

"I don't think he wants to show himself until the last possible minute," Joe muttered. Then he nudged Frank. "There he is now, over there where the gangplank is being hooked up."

The Hardys made their way over to Prynne. He stood waiting, unsmiling.

23

"How are you feeling today?" asked Frank as they joined him.

"Thank you, I feel quite well," said Prynne. He turned back to look at the dock.

Frank kept on. "We didn't want to do anything until we had seen you and talked it over. But I think it's a good idea to report the attack before the guys responsible have a chance to get off the ship and disappear."

Prynne swung around to glare at Frank. "Attack?" he repeated. "I don't know what you're talking about!"

Chapter

4

FRANK AND JOE gave each other a startled glance. "You do remember last night, don't you, Professor?" he said. "The guys who were trying to dump you over the rail? The ones that Chet and I took care of for you? Does any of this ring a bell?"

"If I were you," Prynne answered coldly, "I would put such business completely behind me. The Greek authorities take a dim view of rowdy young people, even young people who carry American passports."

"Rowdy?" Frank exclaimed in disbelief. "Now, wait just a minute! I mean, I don't expect any medals or anything, but I don't call saving you from an attack being 'row-dy'!"

Prynne gave Frank an icy scowl. "Let us get this clear," he said. "For your information, Mr. Hardy, *there was no attack.*"

While Frank gawked, Prynne went on. "Last evening I was suddenly taken with a severe case of seasickness. I felt extremely weak, dizzy, and feverish, and feared that I might pass out. Two passengers very kindly offered to help me outside, where they thought the fresh air might help to revive me.

"No sooner had they assisted me to the deck than we were set upon by two maniacs. Quite understandably, my helpers beat a hasty retreat, frightened out of their wits.

"If I had not felt so wretched, I would have taken you to task then and there for your foolish behavior. Now let's have no further mention of this regrettable affair."

But Frank was not about to let it drop.

"Just a second, Mr. Prynne. What about the third man, who attacked me after we had dealt with the first two? And one of your 'helpers' looked just like one of the 'drunken sailors' who attacked us at the restaurant yesterday. What about that?"

Prynne's eyebrows rose in surprise. "You clearly saw his face?"

"I didn't. But Chet's pretty sure."

"I see," Prynne said with a smirk. "On a dark night, while the two of you were engaged in your disgraceful roughhousing, your friend was 'pretty sure' he recognized a face. Do you expect anyone to believe such a story?"

"But, what about the third man," Joe put in, coming to his brother's aid.

"Ah, yes, the third man," Prynne replied. "As to that, I'm afraid I have nothing to say. Perhaps you tripped over each other in the confusion of the moment. In any event, I strongly suggest that you put this embarrassing matter to rest. That, at least, is what *I* intend to do."

Prynne stalked away, to show that, for him, the subject was closed.

Joe was steaming. "Do you believe anything he said just then?" he demanded.

Frank shook his head. "There's something going on with Prynne, and it's not just seasickness. But if he won't open up, we're out. Let's just keep our eyes open."

After the ship moored, the crew ran down the gangplank and the passengers disembarked. At the foot of the ramp, Frank and Joe noticed a small knot of people waiting to greet them.

The American students circled around the little welcoming group and Morton Prynne performed introductions.

In the middle of the welcomers stood Spiros Stamos, a stocky man with jet black hair and a bushy mustache of the same color. With him was his sixteen-year-old son, Andreas, who was thin and intense, all bones and angles, like a greyhound.

Also on hand was Spiros's seventeen-year-old daughter, Clea. She had her father's glossy black hair, which she wore long and loose. It framed a beautiful face, with golden skin, highlighted by huge dark brown eyes. She was wearing a brightly colored skirt and a snow-white blouse.

When Joe Hardy's turn came to be introduced he shook hands with the father and son, saying he was pleased to meet them.

Then Joe was face-to-face with Clea. He took her hand and said, with his warmest smile, "I'm *really pleased* to meet you."

But Clea just gave him a "How do you do" and an impersonal handshake.

While Peter and his Greek relations embraced and exchanged bits of family news, the other Americans waited to board a bus to the hotel.

Phil moved next to Joe. "Clea is cute—you planning on getting to know her better?"

Joe looked shocked. "Hey, come on. This is a different country, a different culture. You can't just start talking to a girl the way you would at the Bayport Mall. You have to take it slow. Just watch and learn."

Frank walked over then and tugged on Joe's arm, leading him away. "Don't be too obvious about it," he said quietly, "but take a look at the big car by the gangplank. See anyone familiar?"

Joe turned casually to check out the car. He recognized one drab figure moving through the crowd of brightly dressed tourists.

His code name was the Gray Man, and he worked for a supersecret government organization known only as the Network. He was a heavy hitter in the game of international intrigue.

"What's *he* doing here?" Joe wanted to know. "And what was he doing on our ship?"

"Maybe it's a coincidence," replied Frank. But he didn't believe it, and neither did his brother. The Hardys and the Gray Man had crossed paths before. Sometimes they'd helped one another, sometimes they'd found themselves fighting the Network.

Could the Gray Man have been the mysterious rescuer who'd come to Frank's aid last night? If so, why hadn't he made himself known?

Frank watched as the Gray Man got into the large American car and took off.

Frank turned to his brother. "One thing's for sure," he said. "If there's any connection between the Network's business and us, we're involved in something a lot more dangerous than a student tour."

Chapter

5

THE WELCOMING PARTY that evening was a serious party. The crowd of forty seemed to be carrying on about ninety conversations at the same time, and the air was full of shouts, laughter, and music. The tiny Old Quarter restaurant was bulging at the seams.

But from the moment he spotted Clea in the crowd, Joe had eyes and ears for no one else. If she'd looked good that afternoon, she was a knockout that night in a simple linen sleeveless dress.

Joe said to Frank, while never taking his eyes off her, "Is she or isn't she gorgeous?"

Frank had to agree. "Clea's something special, all right. But remember—the kind of stuff that goes over with the girls back home may flop over here. Take your time.''

But Joe had a glow in his eye, and he wasn't about to be steered away from his target. "We're supposed to be getting acquainted, right?" he reasoned with his brother. "Well, I've got some acquainting to do.''

He purposefully moved off through the crowded room.

Clea had been helping one of the Bayport students choose food from the buffet table, but by the time Joe got there, she had vanished into the mob. In her place stood Chet, who was busy getting acquainted with a dozen kinds of Greek noshes.

"You see Clea around?" Joe asked.

"She was here, but she went off that way," Chet replied, gesturing vaguely while maintaining his focus on the goodies. "Hey, Joe, you ought to try some of this stuff. It's good!"

"You must have a dolma," said a female voice on Chet's other side. He looked around to find a pretty girl whose big smile showed off the dimples in her cheeks. She fluttered long eyelashes at Chet, who blinked back uncomfortably.

"I am Alma," she said, taking Chet's plate and adding tidbits to what was already on it.

"Uh, hi. I'm Chet."

"Chet. I like that name. Chet. It's a strong

name, fit for a big man. Here.'' She handed his plate back. ''This is a dolma, a grape leaf stuffed with lamb and rice.''

Chet sampled, and his face lit up. ''Hey, this is great! What's it called again?''

''Dolma. I made it myself. I am a very good cook. One day I will marry a man with a great love of food.''

Chet squirmed, not sure how to reply to the girl. Joe grinned. ''How do you like that? The way to this girl's heart is through *your* stomach.''

Chet glared at Joe, and then turned back to Alma. Before he could think of anything to say to her, his eye met those of a hulking Greek teenager, who stood a few feet behind the girl. He had muscular arms folded across a barrel chest, short, bristly hair, and dark, flashing eyes.

When he saw Chet looking at him, his eyes flashed even more and his face gathered itself into a dark scowl. Chet turned back to Alma.

''Say, um, do you know who that big guy is?'' Chet asked. ''He keeps staring at me.''

Alma looked over, then giggled. ''Oh, that is only my older brother, Aleko. He is—I do not know the word in English—when he sees me with a boy, he is—''

''Jealous?'' inquired Chet faintly.

Alma gave him a brilliant smile. ''Yes, that

is the word. He is very jealous. One time he—Where are you going?"

Chet dove into the thickest part of the crowd, putting as much distance as possible between himself and Alma. Alma frowned and pouted, then followed him. A moment later, the menacing Aleko followed her.

Frank had gotten into conversation with Andreas Stamos, whose initial shyness had given way to enthusiasm when he spoke of the great love of his life—long-distance running.

He announced proudly to Frank, "I'm going to be a marathon runner. Pehaps by 1996 I can compete in the Olympics for my country. I'm the best junior distance runner in Salonika."

Spiros looked down at his son, clearly proud of the boy's achievements. But he only said, "Remember, past accomplishments mean nothing, unless you go on working. All over Greece, all over the world, there are strong, fast boys. Winning will come to the one who wants it the most and tries the hardest."

Andreas grinned. "Every week I run forty to fifty miles."

"Wow—pretty heavy-duty," Peter Stamos said, joining them.

"Next year I'll be running more. When the time comes, I will be ready."

"I bet you will." Frank was deeply impressed by the young runner's determination.

Joe had been making polite chitchat for what seemed like hours, maneuvering to get close to Clea. Every time he got within feet of her, he found himself trapped in another round of introductions. But now, it looked as if his moment had finally arrived. Clea was standing by herself, rearranging the platters of food. Joe walked up to her.

"Can I give you a hand with anything?"

Clea turned toward him, looking at him from those amazing eyes. "No, thank you," she said with a smile. "I've just finished."

Joe toyed with some of the food, picking a few tidbits up and dropping them on a plate. "This is some party your family has put together. You went to a lot of trouble for us."

"To the Greeks, blood ties are important," she said. "This was a very special occasion, our first meeting with our American cousin. Also," she added after a pause, "we wished to give your group a proper welcome."

"Well, speaking for myself," Joe said, "I sure do appreciate it."

Clea continued to smile. "Do you?" she asked sweetly.

"Absolutely." Joe smiled broadly at her.

"Then what I suggest you do," Clea said, "is go to my father and tell him. He is, after all, the one who went to the greatest trouble."

"What I mean is," Joe persisted, "if you

ever feel like going to a movie, or the beach, or for something to eat . . ."

"Ah!" said Clea as the light dawned. *"Now* I understand you. You do not want only to thank me. You want to have what you call a 'date.' "

Joe wondered if he was being laughed at. "Well, yeah."

"You know, Joe, you're not the first American boy to ask me for a date. In your country a young man may approach a girl, even if he hardly knows her, and ask for a date. It is nothing—like picking up a newspaper."

"Well, I wouldn't say that it's nothing," said Joe, feeling his face start to flush.

"No respectable Greek boy would presume to ask such a thing so casually. It shows no respect for the young woman."

"Hey, wait a minute, I didn't mean—"

"While you're here, I hope you take advantage of the opportunity to learn about our customs, about which you clearly know nothing. But don't expect to pick up a girl with a nice smile and sweet words."

Clea walked away, leaving Joe red in the face, openmouthed, and wishing he could crawl under a table.

Now two musicians tuned up their bouzoukis—twangy Greek instruments that looked like a cross between a guitar and a mandolin—

and someone else shouted out, "Give us room to dance!"

Several Greek men began to move in a vigorous, stomping dance, urged on by the clapping of the spectators. They dipped and spun with grace and energy and were clearly having the time of their lives. Their joy in the dance spread to their audience, and even Joe felt his bruised spirits lift. The surging beat of the dancers had brought the party to its height.

And then, without warning, the lights went out.

In the pitch-blackness, a confused babble of voices, Greek and English, arose. Then a shrill scream burst out and was abruptly cut off. There were thumps, as of furniture colliding, then the nasty sound of flesh hitting flesh.

A dim rectangle of light appeared, as the restaurant's front door was opened. Acting on instinct, Frank and Joe both raced for the door. Frank bumped into someone—no telling who in the dark—and tripped over a chair leg. He fell headlong into the space that had been cleared for the dancers.

Joe was luckier than his brother and managed to stay close to the wall, avoiding the chaos of panicky people and fallen objects. He made it to the doorway and dashed into the street, just in time to hear the roar of an engine being revved to its limit. A battered old van screeched around a corner and disappeared into the night.

A moment later some order was restored. Lanterns were found and lit. Frank picked himself up as Joe returned.

"You see anything?"

"Just a beat-up old van taking a corner on two wheels. You okay?"

"Yeah," Frank answered, dusting off his clothes. "I just got blindsided by a chair."

"Peter! Peter!" Andreas was shouting wildly. *"Peter!* Where is he?"

Spiros Stamos took his son by the shoulders to calm him. "What about Peter?" he asked.

"He—he was just here, with me! I was talking to him when the lights went out, and now he's gone!"

The restaurant was small and a thorough search took little time. When it was over, there could be no doubt: Peter Stamos had disappeared.

Chapter

6

IT WAS QUITE late now, and the restaurant had been cleared up. The electric lights were back on—the intruders had simply unscrewed a fuse from the box outside. Local police had arrived on the scene, questioning Spiros Stamos, Kaliotis, and Prynne, then departed.

The American students had all gone back to their hotel, a little scared and a lot shaken—all except for Frank and Joe Hardy. They'd stayed behind. Now they were approaching Morton Prynne, who stood off by himself, looking tired and drawn.

When he saw the Hardys moving toward him, he gave them his trademark cold stare.

"What are you doing here?" he demanded.

"I told you students to head back to the hotel and get some sleep."

"Well, we decided that this would be a perfect time for a heart-to-heart talk," replied Frank, crossing his arms over his chest.

"Now, look here, you two," snapped Prynne. "I am in no mood for nonsense."

"Nonsense!" Joe was indignant. "Maybe there's been nonsense going on around here, but we're not the ones responsible for it! The time's come for you to level with us."

"I don't know what you're babbling about," insisted Prynne.

"Number one," said Frank, "the 'incident' at lunch yesterday, when we were attacked by supposedly drunken sailors. Number two, the two guys who wanted to help you get rid of your seasickness—permanently. And now, Peter gets snatched by someone. I'm beginning to get a little suspicious. Two attempts on you, one on the nephew of our host. And you're trying to tell us there's no connection?"

"You may think we're rude and rowdy," added Joe, "but don't think we're stupid."

"Come on, Mr. Prynne," Frank urged. "Tell us what's going on. You never know. We might be able to help."

"Help! You think you can help? You're just a pair of fools!" Clea Stamos advanced on them, her eyes flashing in anger.

"What do you know of our country?" she demanded. "You Americans, you make me sick! Your interference in matters you cannot understand might cause my cousin's death. Don't give us your 'help,' please. Mind your own business and let us mind ours."

"Clea!" Spiros Stamos came forward and put an arm around his daughter, gently drawing her away from the Hardys and Prynne. "It is time you were at home. Come with me."

Clea sagged back against her father, closing her eyes and allowing herself to be led away. Spiros waved a good-night to the three Americans as he left the restaurant with his daughter.

Prynne took a deep breath before saying to Frank and Joe, "Come on, you two. I have a taxi waiting."

Sitting in the cab, the three remained silent during the short drive to the hotel. But as they reached the hotel lobby, Frank stepped in front of Prynne.

"You have nothing to say to us?" he asked.

"All I have to say has already been said," Prynne replied. "You're making something out of nothing."

Joe now spoke up. "Okay, in that case let's just add one last piece of nothing to the picture. This afternoon, Frank and I saw an old friend get off our ship and into a car at the pier—the Gray Man.''

Prynne stared at them, his eyes narrowed. ''The Gray Man?''

Frank continued, ''That's his code name— what everyone calls him in the Network.''

Prynne's suspicion had now given way to amazement. ''You—you are familiar with the Network?'' he asked at length.

Frank and Joe smiled at Prynne. ''What's more,'' said Joe, *''they* are familiar with *us.''*

''We *do* get around, you know,'' added Frank.

Morton Prynne stared at them, took off his glasses, and wiped them on his handkerchief. He said, ''I can't tell you anything—not tonight at least. Be patient for tonight and let's plan to have breakfast together tomorrow. Perhaps then I can say more.''

''Tomorrow morning then,'' Frank agreed. ''But we'll be expecting some hard facts and not just a lot of smoke.''

Prynne just nodded and headed for his room.

The following morning found Frank, Joe, and Prynne sitting at a table in the hotel café. Prynne had not said much, and the Hardys were getting annoyed.

It was Joe who broke the long silence. ''Listen," he said, rattling a juice glass on the tile table, "if breakfast was all you had in mind here, I'd just as soon have slept a little later."

Prynne held up a hand. "No, no," he protested, "it's simply that . . . I think we'd better have our little talk someplace more private. I'm going to my room. You wait here for five minutes, looking around to see if anyone follows me out. If it's all clear, then come up and join me. Understood?"

Frank's eyebrows raised. "Is this really necessary?"

Prynne got up and surveyed the Hardys. "Once we've had our talk," he replied, "you can judge that for yourselves."

Joe and Frank knocked on Prynne's door and were quickly motioned inside. As they sat down, Frank said, "No one followed you, and as far as I can tell, no one followed us. Let's talk."

Prynne paced nervously for a moment, then stopped and faced the Hardys. "Everything I am about to tell you is highly confidential—not a word of this can be repeated. Is that clear?"

Joe nodded. "We know all about the Network's security."

"Very well," Prynne answered. "First of all, I *am* an operative of the Network.

"We have an agent who has been working under deep cover in various nations of the

Eastern Bloc, gathering sensitive military information. His code name is Atlas. Right now, he's making his way through Yugoslavia. Tomorrow he will reach the Greek-Yugoslavian border."

"In other words," Frank cut in, "he may be within forty miles of here."

Prynne nodded. "Essentially correct, although the spot will be more like sixty by the mountain roads. My assignment was to lead a small force to get him back across the border, back to the West. Since being a professor is my usual cover, they put me in charge of a student tour to Greece."

Joe started to his feet, but Prynne waved him back down. "I'm not happy about using innocent students as part of an operation like this— but the decision was not mine.

"Upon our arrival here, American and Greek groups were to join together, under Spiros Stamos—our Network contact. He would take them on a tour, well away from the scene of the action, while I went north with my people to get Atlas."

"And then the wheels fell off your little wagon," Frank observed.

Prynne winced. "You put it crudely, but that's true. Our cover seems to have been completely blown. You were right, of course, seeing the connection between the attacks."

He shook his head. "Before we got to Greece, two key Greek operatives were taken out. The body of one was found two days ago, and the other has yet to be heard from. These men were supposed to go north with me. I'm planning to take Spiros now, but even so it will—"

A knock on the door stopped him. Prynne opened it to admit a very worried Spiros Stamos. He nodded a greeting to the Hardys and said to Prynne, "We must talk."

"Certainly, Spiros, sit down."

Stamos turned to Frank and Joe. "Boys, I must speak privately with Mr. Prynne, if you would not mind leaving for—"

"No, no, Spiros, it's all right," interrupted Prynne. "These young men seem to have known almost from the beginning that things weren't normal. What's more, when our friend got off the ship yesterday, they recognized him. They know about the Network and his connection with it."

Stamos stared at Frank and Joe. "How is it possible that these boys should know of such things?"

"Let's just say that we've gotten caught up in a couple of Network deals before," Joe replied. "It wouldn't do to go into the details, would it?"

"No, no, certainly not," Prynne agreed

quickly. "But, Spiros, you can speak in front of these two, and we must rely on their continued discretion. What have you come to tell me?"

Stamos walked to the window and stood looking out. "Very early this morning," he said with his back to the others in the room, "I had a telephone call from the ones who are holding Peter. They told me, if I wished to see the boy alive again, I must take no further part in what they called 'foolish criminal activities.' "

Stamos turned from the window and looked at Morton Prynne, the burden of a painful decision showing clearly in his face.

"Morton," he said, "at first I was supposed to do nothing more than lead a student tour—simple and hardly dangerous. Then, last night we talked about my joining you in place of one of the men we lost. This meant some risk, but I was willing to do it, because I believe in the cause.

"Now the danger is not mine alone. I do not fear to lay my life on the line if need be. You understand this. I am not a coward."

"Of course you're not, Spiros," said Prynne quietly. "No one could think such a thing."

"You must see, then," Stamos went on, staring fixedly at Prynne, "that I no longer have a choice in this matter. I cannot allow harm to come to the son of my brother, while he is in my care."

He hung his head. "That is why I cannot go to the border with you."

Chapter

7

"IT LOOKS LIKE you guys could use a little help," said Frank.

"And it just happens that our calendar is clear," continued Joe.

Prynne stared at the brothers in shock. "Are you two actually suggesting that you become actively involved in this business?"

"It did cross our minds," answered Frank.

"It'd sure beat touring ruins," replied Joe.

Spiros Stamos pulled a chair close to the Hardys and sat down. "Boys, we are dealing with very dangerous opponents. They won't hesitate to kill anyone who stands in their way."

He gave them a hard look. "Understand—as

long as they see you as students, you won't be harmed. They wouldn't dare create an international incident. But if it were known that you are members of our team, your youth would not protect you. You'd become targets."

Prynne jumped in. "Moreover, I don't have the authority to bring you in. I can't be responsible for exposing you to harm."

"Now, don't be too hasty," protested Frank. "I can see you think we're just kids who want to play cops and robbers and get in your way. I don't expect that we can convince you otherwise, not by ourselves."

"But if our old buddy, the Gray Man, is around, he can vouch for us," Joe said. "I know he can approve our coming aboard. So that'd take you off the hook, Mr. Prynne."

Prynne angrily blurted, "I don't care about being 'on the hook,' young man! I have a legitimate concern about your safety. However—wait here." He left the room.

"He probably has to get permission to change neckties," said Joe.

Stamos gave Joe an angry look. "I think that Morton Prynne might well surprise you," he said. "There's more to him than what you perceive."

Only a few minutes passed before Prynne returned with the Hardys' old acquaintance.

The Gray Man was not overjoyed to see Frank and Joe.

"If I had the slightest idea that you two might be included in this group," he said sourly, "I would have scrubbed the whole operation."

"Well, things go wrong." Frank looked at the agent. "By the way, do I owe you for a helping hand on the ship the other night? If it was you, then thanks."

The Gray Man waved it off. "Let's call that an even trade," he said. "After all, you were helping Mr. Prynne out of an awkward scrape."

"Look," Joe cut in, "I don't think you have any gripes about us being around to help. You need us now, and you've got us."

That got him a glare from the Gray Man. "We do *not* need you! Just because you've managed to keep from getting killed so far doesn't mean that you're trained agents. We'll get by without you."

"Is that a fact?" Joe asked. "Seems to me you've dug yourselves into a nice, deep hole so far. I don't see how we could possibly make things any worse."

"If this operation is as important as you say," Frank went on, "you have a problem getting a new team in here. We have a couple of friends here who are also very good in a crunch. Phil Cohen is a genius with anything electronic or technical, and Chet Morton may not look it, but he can be tough when it really counts. So—what do you say?''

The Gray Man simmered. They had him in a bind. The loss of Atlas would be a disaster, and almost as bad would be any public exposure of a Network fiasco. He thought hard for a second, and then spoke to Frank and Joe.

"Your analysis of our predicament may be a little overstated, but not too far off the mark. We don't have many options. But if we're going to try to pull this off, I have a few ground rules. First, you'll follow orders—exactly. Second, if it appears that you are in any immediate physical danger you'll stop whatever you are doing and bail out. At once. Agreed?''

Frank and Joe glanced at each other, then looked, with solemn faces, back at the Gray Man.

"Of course," said Frank.

"Makes sense to me," said Joe.

"Very well then," said the Gray Man.

Spiros Stamos came forward. "My children Clea and Andreas are concerned about their cousin and wish to help. Also, the girl Alma and her brother Aleko are closely tied to our family. I am Alma's godfather. And Nicholas Kaliotis will want to be of service as well."

The Gray Man frowned. "Kaliotis? What's his connection?"

"Nicholas was practically raised by my father," replied Stamos. "We are the only family he has. For a Greek, ties of family are sacred."

Taking Stamos's hand in both of his, Prynne said, "Thank you for your suggestions, Spiros. We will consider them. Now, go home. We will keep you informed."

After the Gray Man and Stamos departed, Chet and Phil were summoned to Prynne's room and briefed on what was happening and why.

"Here's the plan," said Prynne. "I'll lead a group north to the border rendezvous. We'll pass ourselves off as a teacher of classical history and his students—there are archaeological digs and a ruined fortress not far from the scheduled meet.

"We'll go with tools—picks, shovels, and the like—as well as some explosives. My party will include Joe, Phil, whose technical know-how may be of use, and Andreas, since we must have one Greek-speaker along.

"Frank, Chet, and the rest will begin a search for Peter Stamos. The other students will be taken on an innocent tour, to keep them out of danger, and fed a story to account for the absence of those of you who will be working with us. Any questions?"

No one had anything to add. The group broke up to make arrangements, get supplies, and pass on information to those who had not been present. At dinnertime they'd meet again at the hotel.

That evening found Frank, Joe, Prynne, Chet, Phil, and Kaliotis around the dinner table. Andreas, who was expected, had not yet arrived.

"We'll start without him," Prynne decided, pulling out a checklist. "Those of you going with me must be ready to leave by six A.M. I've gotten an all-terrain vehicle, just in case any problems force us to leave the main road.

"We'll take along a multiband radio receiver-transmitter, and we'll call in regularly. The Salonika party will have a similar radio. Listen for our calls every hour on the hour. When we have reached—"

Chet, who was facing the entrance to the restaurant, cut in on Prynne's instructions: "Here's Andreas."

Joe turned toward the door and frowned. "Here comes trouble," he said.

Andreas was not alone. At his side, with her jaw set and a challenge in her eyes, walked his sister. Andreas could hardly look at the people around the table, stammering, "She made me tell her what we are doing. She wants to . . . I couldn't . . ."

Clea spoke up. "I am going to the border too. If my brother can go, then I can as well."

"Now, wait a second," said Joe, holding up his hands. "There's plenty that you can do here in Salonika, Clea. From what Mr. Prynne says, we could find ourselves in rough country. We can't be held up by—by someone who isn't physically up to the job."

"Not up to it!" Clea's eyes shot fire at Joe. "Why do you assume that? I have spent much time in the places you are going, camping and climbing mountains."

She pointed to her brother. "Do you think *he* can keep up, because he is a boy? On flat ground, he can outrun me. But in the mountains, he is no match for me. And this way you will have another Greek along."

Joe glared, but Morton Prynne cut the debate off. "Very well, Clea, we have room in the truck, and you may join us. But understand, no allowances will be made for you if it becomes necessary to go on foot. You will be expected to keep up to our pace."

Clea smiled. "You do not have to worry about me," she said.

They were running through the final preparations when a waiter came through the room, calling Frank's name. Frank raised his hand. "Over here!"

"Mr. Frank Hardy? You are wanted on the telephone in the lobby."

Going to the booth, Frank picked up the phone.

"Hello?"

"Frank Hardy?" The voice was accented, unfamiliar. "Here is someone who wishes to speak to you."

After a momentary pause, another voice came on the line, shaky and very frightened.

"Frank?"

"Peter! Is that you?"

"Yeah, it's me. I have—"

"Listen, how are you doing? You okay?"

"I—I'm all right. A little shook up, but they haven't hurt me—yet. I'm supposed to give you a message from them."

"Go ahead, Peter."

"They say that you'd better not go ahead with your mission. You can't succeed. If you try, they'll—they'll kill me. They really mean it, Frank. I'm scared."

"Listen, Peter." Frank tried to make his voice a lot more confident and reassuring than he felt. "Take it easy. We'll get you out of this. We won't let anything happen to you. Understand?"

"Yeah, I guess."

Frank racked his brains, trying to think of

some way to keep Peter on the line and maybe pick up clues to his whereabouts.

"Listen, Peter, I want to ask you a few questions, if they'll let you stay on the line. Just answer yes or no. Got it?"

"Yes."

"Are you still in the city?"

But the only response was a sudden dry click.

Frank's knuckles whitened as he tightened his grip on the phone.

"Peter? Peter! You there?"

No answer.

Frank stared in helpless frustration at the dead receiver.

Chapter
8

By SEVEN-THIRTY the following morning, the all-terrain vehicle, with Prynne at the wheel, had left Salonika far behind. Joe Hardy rode shotgun, with Phil Cohen, Andreas, and Clea Stamos in back, along with their gear—extra clothes, tools, and an emergency supply of gasoline.

The road had been straight and wide at first. But now they were going with some care along a twisting, two-lane ribbon of concrete that clung to a mountainside, full of hairpin turns. On one side they were hemmed in by a steep, rocky slope covered with boulders and scraggly bushes. On the other side was a dizzying drop into a deep gorge.

"Not much traffic on this road," Joe observed.

"It's too early in the day," answered Clea, leaning over the front seat. "Anyway, there is not much ahead on this road except the border, some ruins, and that old Turkish fortress."

"How come a Turkish fortress?" Phil wanted to know.

"The Turks ruled here for quite a long time," Prynne explained from behind the wheel. "So did the Venetians, the Franks, and various other groups over the years."

"Until we won our independence," Andreas added with pride.

Suddenly a large Mercedes sedan appeared behind them, moving much faster than they were. Prynne edged the ATV to the right, and the luxurious car glided past, quickly putting distance between them. The windows were so darkly tinted that it was impossible to see inside.

Phil whistled as they watched the Mercedes vanish around a curve ahead. "Pretty fast for a tricky stretch like this."

"Oh, I don't know," Joe answered. "A car like that has a low center of gravity and great suspension. Now, if you took *this* baby at that speed—"

"I don't even want to think about it," Phil said, with a shake of his head. "I have this strange fear of falling several hundred feet into a dry riverbed. Some hang-up, huh?"

Joe laughed as they whipped through a demanding set of mountain turns. Then, coming around on one especially sharp turn, they found the Mercedes that had passed them. It was parked diagonally across the road, blocking both lanes.

Prynne braked with a squeal of tires. Almost before they had stopped, a series of shots rang out from somewhere above them. A webbed hole appeared in the windshield, and a metallic clank indicated a bullet striking the body of the truck somewhere.

"Ambush!" shouted Joe.

"Turn around!" Andreas screamed.

"No room." Prynne threw the ATV into reverse and lurched away from the trap. More shots rang out as Prynne made the treacherous hairpin turn backward. About two hundred yards farther along he slowed the vehicle and backed it off the paved surface and into a cleft in the rock, protected on either side by almost vertical cliffs.

"Phil, get on that radio, and let the people back in Salonika know we've been attacked," Prynne ordered. "The rest of you, start looking for shelter. I imagine we'll have company soon, and we know they're well-armed."

"Andreas, Clea, let's move!" urged Joe, who was already out of the truck.

Behind the truck, the cleft ran deeper into the rocks but didn't seem to be more than a blind alley.

Phil had set the radio up and was listening with a frown to the static coming out of the speaker. "The mountains are blocking us here," he said. "I tried to send word, but I don't know if anything's getting out or *to* us." He turned up the receiver, which hissed with the static.

"Keep trying," Joe said, coming back and shaking his head. "It doesn't look like we've got much in the way of shelter here," he advised Prynne. "These cliffs are steep, and I don't see where—"

"Joe! Come here!" called Clea. "I think there is a place up there."

Joe ran over to her and followed her pointing finger, but all he saw was what appeared to be a slight break in a sheer cliff. He told her as much.

"You don't have a mountaineer's eye," she said impatiently. "I will show you."

She began to climb up quickly, finding little crevices for her hands and feet. About fifteen feet above them, she pulled herself up onto a ledge and looked down to the others.

"This is wide enough to hide us," she called down.

Prynne ordered Andreas to climb up, help his sister look for possible weapons, and stockpile them.

"What kind of weapons?" Andreas wanted to know. "We have no guns." Prynne had ordered them not to have guns in case they were caught. The guns would blow their cover.

"Rocks," replied Prynne. "Good throwing rocks."

"Rocks against guns?" Andreas muttered.

"They're all we have now," Prynne replied.

Andreas scrambled up to join Clea. Joe came back to Prynne. "I may have an idea," he said, explaining quickly.

Prynne nodded. "Set it up," he said. "I'm going to explore farther up into the cleft."

Joe ordered Phil to stow the radio, and gave him a length of rope, but Phil still looked at the steep rock face unhappily.

"Look, if Clea can do it, then *we* can do it," coaxed Joe. "It's not completely smooth, like glass. Look for little ridges, little cracks, use the plants for handholds. It's better than just sitting here and waiting for them."

With this encouragement, Phil carefully started up, the rope slung over his shoulder. With Clea shouting instructions and urging him on, Phil slowly got to the ledge, where he rolled himself onto the flat surface with a deep sigh of relief.

Then they hauled up a bundle of spare clothes and a can of gasoline. Morton Prynne came out from the inner reaches of the cleft, and Joe stopped to check with him.

"We're ready to go up there," he said. "Are you coming?"

"I've found a little hiding place back there," replied Prynne, gesturing with his thumb. "It's a kind of mini-cave that'll hold just me. It's better that someone stays on ground level, so we attack from two directions at once. Watch for my signal, and then let 'em have it."

Joe grinned at Prynne and said, "Well, here goes nothing." He started up the ledge, while the other man retreated into the crevice.

On the ledge, Joe found a good-size pile of rocks being gathered. He tied the spare clothes into bundles, soaking them in gasoline. Each makeshift torch also got a rock for throwing weight.

Phil studied them, then asked Joe, "Think these'll do any damage?"

"Well, they'll surprise whoever they're dropped on. Maybe that'll give us an edge."

Preparations finished, the four students lay in wait on their ledge, with Prynne below, tucked into his little niche. Minutes dragged by, and the silence was complete. It grew warm on the ledge, and Joe wiped the sweat from his eyes.

Then, a man's head peered cautiously around from the road. The scout saw the ATV, and called back over his shoulder. Seconds later, four men were standing near the truck, searching. The four above flattened themselves down and froze.

Joe whispered to Phil, "Those guns they have are AK-forty-sevens. Russian-made, automatic."

Phil whispered back, "How'll they stand up against manually operated Greek rocks?"

Joe nudged Clea. "What are those guys saying?"

"I don't know," she whispered back. "They aren't speaking Greek."

One of the gunmen now moved out of sight, down the road from where the Mercedes sat, off to see if the ATV passengers had fled in that direction.

"That cuts the odds down a little," Joe muttered. "Get ready."

Prynne leapt from his cover, landing on the back of the nearest opponent and clamping an arm around his throat. The other two wheeled around, but as they did, the four on the ledge hurled a hail of rocks, some of them trailing flaming torches. One of the men was smashed squarely in the side of the head and toppled.

The other had his aim spoiled when a torch nearly singed his face. He jerked away, only to have Joe drop from the ledge onto him.

The AK-47 fell to the ground. Joe lunged for the gun, but was grabbed from behind. Twisting, Joe saw that his man had him by the leg with one hand, while reaching for a knife with the other.

Joe kicked back with his free leg, catching the man hard in the chest and breaking his grip. A quick roll brought Joe to his feet. But his opponent, knife in hand, barred the way to the gun.

A wild slash sent Joe stepping back, looking for more room. But his foot landed in a shallow hole and he tumbled, landing hard. Sensing his chance for a quick kill, the thug started forward, but a sudden burst of automatic weapon fire from behind froze him in his tracks.

There stood Phil, glaring over the sights of the AK-47 in his hands. Joe's attacker dropped his knife and raised his hands. "Joe, you all right?" Phil asked.

"Can't complain," Joe said, getting up and dusting himself off. "Much obliged for the help."

"Any time."

Clea and Andreas by now had made their descent from the ledge, and Prynne stood alone, cradling an AK-47. At his feet lay another thug, lying flat out before him.

"Is he—dead?" Andreas asked in a shaky voice.

"No, just fast asleep. I didn't cut off his air supply long enough to do him any serious damage," Prynne said calmly. "Joe, pick up that gun, if you would, and then we'll wait for the fourth one, who should be here before long."

A few minutes later they heard a voice calling out a question in the same mysterious language their attackers had used. To the surprise of all the others, Prynne called out an equally unintelligible response.

A moment afterward the fourth attacker strolled into the recess, to find three AK-47s pointed right at him. Sensibly, he lowered his gun and joined his comrades.

The four disarmed gunmen were pulled back into the deeper part of the cleft in the rocks, where they were tied securely with rope and their own belts. While this went on, Joe asked Prynne, "What was that language you were speaking?"

"Serbo-Croatian," Prynne replied, his eyes still on the prisoners. "Phil, that rope needs tightening. That's more like it."

"You speak Serbo-Croatian?"

"I'm a bit rusty," Prynne said, smiling, "but good enough for the present purposes."

While the others finished with their captives, Phil and Joe headed for the ATV to try the radio again. As they neared the truck, Joe stopped short, noticing a pool of liquid spreading out from under the front end. He ran to the front of the vehicle and knelt down. Then he raised the hood and looked down at the engine. Phil joined him.

"What's up?" Phil wanted to know.

Scowling, Joe thumped the motor. "Look for yourself. We took a bullet in the radiator, and this engine is scrap metal. We're not going anywhere—at least not in this truck."

Chapter
9

WAITING, FRANK THOUGHT, is the hardest
thing of all, especially while somebody else is
out doing something. He and Chet, along with
Alma and Aleko, sat in Frank's hotel room. He
kept checking his watch, amazed at how slowly
the time crawled along.

The multiband radio sat on the bureau. But
the time to check for messages hadn't arrived
yet, nor had Nicholas Kaliotis. Frank went
back over the events of the past few days in his
head.

Suddenly he sat up straight, and said, "Hey,
I just remembered something from last night."

"Let's hear it," Chet exclaimed.

"Well," Frank went on, "while I was on the

phone with Peter, when he was giving me the word from the people holding him, I heard—I think it was a whistle. Yeah, like a boat whistle! Maybe that could help to narrow down the areas to search.''

Aleko sighed and shook his head sadly. "In Salonika, you can hear whistles from ships almost anywhere. It is no help.''

Frank slumped back in his chair. Finally he went over to turn on the radio.

"Phil should be in touch any minute now,'' he said. But the only sound to emerge was static. He turned the volume all the way up and paced the floor. Nothing. In frustration, he slammed the bureau top with the flat of his hand.

"You're sure that's the right frequency?'' Chet asked.

Frank glared at him. "It's the right frequency, the right time, the right everything. Maybe—''

"Shhh!'' hissed Alma, bending close to the radio's speaker. "Listen!''

Through the interference Phil's voice could just be made out, barely audible: "Ambushed . . . trapped on . . . road . . . automatic weapons . . . careful . . .'' The static swelled, and the faint voice disappeared altogether. Frank attempted a transmission.

"Base to Northern Group . . . Base to Northern Group . . . Do you read me, Northern Group? . . . Phil, are you there? Over. Come in if you read me, Phil, over." But the only sound from the receiver was noise.

"Ambushed!" Frank snapped. "The other side was waiting for them up there. Someone's been one step ahead of us every move we've made."

There was a knock on the door, and Aleko opened it to admit Nicholas Kaliotis, who was immediately surrounded by Frank and the others in the room.

"We heard from Phil. They've been ambushed on the road by guys with machine guns!"

"We've got to do something fast!"

"Have you heard anything about Peter? Is he alive?"

"Listen, we have to get reinforcements up toward the border, they may be—"

"Quiet!" Nicholas's roar cut through the excited barrage. "Now, one at a time, if you please. Did you actually speak to them?"

"No, the interference was terrible," Frank replied. "We were able to make out bits and pieces and then we lost them completely. I tried responding, but I don't think I got through."

"Hmmm. Yes, in the mountains, radio reception might be difficult," said Kaliotis. "But you were able to establish that they were under attack of some kind?"

"The first word we heard was *ambushed*," Chet exclaimed.

"How quickly can you organize a relief party?" asked Frank. "They may not have much time."

Kaliotis cut off the discussion. "Right," he said. "Stay here for a few minutes. I will be back as soon as I can. I must see to getting a team prepared to go north. Wait." And he was gone.

Frank picked up where he had left off before the arrival of Kaliotis. "I can't see any other explanation for it," he said, flopping back onto the couch. "Somebody is passing information to the other side."

"But—but who?" Alma asked.

"Well, they took out two Greek agents before we arrived in the country," Frank answered. "That suggests the leak is someone from over here. I think we can eliminate Stamos and his family." And then noticing that Aleko looked ready to erupt, he added, "And we also can cross off those who are very close to the family." Aleko subsided.

"But what about Kaliotis? What's his story?"

Alma spoke up. "It could not be him. When he was a young boy his father and mother were killed in the civil war by Communist partisans. The partisans also kidnapped thousands of children over the border into the East. His only brother was taken away, never to be seen or heard from again. Spiros Stamos's father raised Nicholas as one of his own. They are the only family he has. It is not possible that he could betray them."

"Okay, if you say so," Frank said, as he stood and began to pace again. "But we have a weak link somewhere. So we'd all better be careful about who we talk to until we clear it up."

Alma's face was serious until she caught Chet's eye and gave him a beaming smile.

"It is a frightening thing that we are dealing with, but I feel lucky to have such strong, brave men to help us. Have you been involved in such matters before?"

Chet shifted his feet, looked at Frank and then away, and mumbled, "Not *real* often— not at all, hardly. Well, maybe a little."

Frank put a hand on Chet's shoulder. "Alma," Frank told her gravely, "you're looking at a real hero. Why, he saved my life once already this trip, and two days ago, I saw him take a knife away from a vicious criminal."

Alma's eyes gleamed. "I knew it," she whispered. "A tiger."

"Come on, Frank," Chet muttered, squirming in his chair. "Cut it out, will you?"

"Alma!" Aleko rumbled, giving her a dark scowl. "Enough of this foolishness! This is not the time or place."

There was a quiet tap on the door, and Kaliotis stepped inside. "We must leave at once. I have taken the necessary steps," he said. "Now we'll go to where the group is preparing to leave, but we must hurry. On the way, I will tell you what has been learned about Peter's present whereabouts. Hurry!"

The group followed him outside and piled into an elderly Volvo.

Kaliotis headed away from the newer, central district of Salonika and toward the waterfront. The areas they went through became shabbier and shabbier.

"Where are we headed?" asked Frank.

"It is what is called a 'safe house,' " said Kaliotis. "There we are gathering those who will go to help your brother, and there we will make our plans to rescue Peter Stamos. We will be there soon."

Shortly afterward they pulled up in front of a seedy, run-down building with metal shutters covering its windows. The stucco walls had faded until it was impossible to tell what color they had been.

"This is it?" Chet looked doubtful.

"This is it," answered Kaliotis. "You don't want a safe house to call attention to itself, do you? This place blends with its neighbors."

"That doesn't say much for the neighborhood," noted Chet as he and Frank left the car. With Kaliotis in the lead, they entered a dim hallway. Kaliotis opened a narrow door and stood back, gesturing them in.

"Be careful going down the stairs," he cautioned. "They are steep and the light is poor."

Frank led the way down the flight of creaky steps and into a cellar lit only by a couple of low-wattage bulbs in wall sockets. They found a number of men cleaning and loading pistols and automatic weapons.

"Looks like you've got a real task force here," Frank observed to Kaliotis.

Then his eyes fell on what seemed to be a bundle of clothes piled on the floor against a wall. As his eyes got used to the lack of light, Frank realized with a jolt that he was staring at the bound and gagged body of Peter Stamos.

Frank spun around to discover that most of the guns in the room were now aimed at him and his friends. Kaliotis had led them directly into the hands of the opposition!

Chapter

10

Prynne, Joe, Phil, Clea, and Andreas stared unhappily at the ruined ATV. Joe slammed down the hood. "We need new wheels," he said.

Prynne took off his glasses and wiped them with a handkerchief. "There's a very nice Mercedes just around the corner," he said.

Phil shook his head. "There'll be guards—and I'll bet they won't be ready to lend it to us."

"Then I guess we'll have to persuade them. Got any ideas?" Joe turned to Prynne.

The agent shook his head. "The problem is getting close enough without getting shot."

Joe took Prynne's arm, leading him back to

where their four prisoners lay tied. Joe pointed to one of them. "He looks just about my size. With his clothes and that knit cap of his to cover my hair, I could pass for him."

"Maybe at a distance," Prynne said dubiously, looking at the prisoner's stubbly face.

"We could all walk around the curve with me holding you at gunpoint as captives," Joe went on. "We'd get as close as possible to the Mercedes, then all we'd need was some sort of distraction to let us rush the guards."

Joe smiled. "Phil could make a very loud distraction with the explosives in the ATV. Let me try this guy's outfit on for size."

When Prynne and Joe walked back to the others, Joe was wearing a pair of baggy khaki pants, a grimy black sweatshirt, and a black knit cap.

"Well, what do you think?" he asked.

"As a fashion statement," said Phil, "it's the pits. Is there a point to this?"

Joe swiftly outlined his strategy, then turned to Phil. "We need an explosion—something with a lot of noise and smoke but no damage. It should go off forty-five seconds from the time we start walking toward the Mercedes."

Phil examined the area, marking a spot with his toe. "About here, you'd get lots of echo, and it'd be harmless."

"Excellent," Prynne said. "You stay here,

with one of the AK-forty-sevens. When your explosion goes, fire a few short bursts, just to add to the noise and general confusion. After that, act at your own discretion. Understood?"

Phil nodded and went to work.

"You know," Joe said, "it would be a good idea if I knew a few words in their language."

"Serbo-Croatian." Prynne nodded. "Let's see, I'll teach you. 'It's all right, these are prisoners,' and 'Help! Come quickly!' That'll be enough for our purposes."

While Prynne was drilling the phrases into Joe, Clea came up with a handful of mud, which she smeared over Joe's cheeks, jaws, and chin.

"It will look like the face of an unshaven man, from perhaps thirty yards," she said.

Joe shrugged. "If we get that close and Phil's bomb hasn't gone off, we're in trouble anyway."

"It's ready." Phil picked up his AK-47.

"Right." Prynne started out of the cleft. "Phil, we'll be expecting your explosion forty-five seconds from when we go around the turn."

"You got it," Phil answered. "Good luck, guys."

A moment later, Prynne, Clea, and Andreas appeared around the curve, their hands clasped behind their heads. Joe came just behind, carrying an AK-47 and muttering his two Serbo-Croatian phrases under his breath. The Mercedes stood about one hundred and fifty yards away, with two men guarding it.

"Slow down," hissed Prynne. "We don't want to get too close too soon."

The guards had by now caught sight of them. One yelled something.

"Don't answer yet," whispered Prynne. "Make a show of not being able to hear him."

On they trudged, and the guard called out once more and brought his gun up to his shoulder.

Joe waved one arm over his head and shouted out what he hoped would pass for assurance that everything was all right. The guard lowered his gun and called out something else.

"What's he saying now?" whispered Joe.

"He wants to know where the others are. Try the first phrase again."

Joe repeated the first line as they moved steadily closer.

Fifty yards. The guard shouted out more sharply, and both men now trained their AK-47s on the approaching group.

Forty yards. Suddenly the roar of an explosion filled the air, followed by the rattle of an automatic weapon.

Joe spun around, yelling to the alarmed

guards. He kept his face turned away and fired a couple of short bursts in the general direction of the blast. The three "prisoners" moved aside.

The two guards came running up. Joe let the first go past, then tackled the second man. He caught him at knee level from behind, cutting him down and sending the man's AK-47 skittering away.

The other guard turned back, his gun wavering as he tried to find a shot that wouldn't hit his comrade. Before the guard had a clear shot, Prynne rushed in to knock the gun aside. The man pulled free but Prynne drove a shoulder into him, sending both of them sprawling into a gully.

Meanwhile Joe tried to pin his man, but the gunman kicked out, sending Joe flying. After a bone-jarring landing, Joe struggled to rise. He turned to see that the guard was scrambling for his fallen AK-47. With a desperate lunge, Joe caught the man's foot, and Clea darted in to snatch up the weapon.

The man now tried to kick loose and grab for Clea, but Andreas jumped in, kicking him hard as he could in the stomach. The guy sagged to the ground, while Joe took the AK-47 from Clea and covered him.

"Where is Mr. Prynne?" Clea asked, "and that other man?"

"I was hoping *someone* would ask," came Prynne's voice from alongside the road. They peered into the ditch. There lay the gunman. On top of him sat Prynne, holding a gun.

"Way to go, Mr. Prynne!" Joe exclaimed, as Phil came running up.

"How are you all doing up there?" Phil wanted to know.

"Everything's under control," Joe replied. Prynne looked up at the students, and they suddenly noticed that he was pale and sweaty. "My leg," Prynne said. "I think I've torn a ligament in my ankle. That means I won't be doing any long-distance walking for some time. Could someone give me a hand?"

Joe helped Prynne over to the Mercedes, while the others took the guards to join their fellow captives. Then, taking the radio and the captured guns, they piled into the liberated car and resumed their northward journey with Joe at the wheel.

Prynne watched the barren countryside roll by for a while and then spoke up. "What worries me now is that whoever set up that ambush is likely to take another shot at us. I wish we could get off this main route."

From the back seat, Clea spoke up. "There is an old road leading directly to the ruined fort."

"Our rendezvous is an abandoned shepherd's hut, right on the border," Prynne said. "Do you know it?"

"I don't know the cabin," admitted Clea. "But it should not be hard to find."

Prynne sighed. "I had hoped to make that hike myself, but under the circumstances Joe will have to undertake it, if he's willing."

"It'll be a pleasure," Joe said with a grin. "Clean mountain air, beautiful scenery—and I've never seen Yugoslavia. I wouldn't miss it."

"And *I* will go with you," announced Clea.

Before Joe could protest, Prynne nodded. "You'll need a guide," he said. "But there is the possibility of a great risk."

"Don't worry, Mr. P.," Joe answered, "I'll look after her."

Clea smiled. "We will look after each other."

The road began to climb until at the crest of a hill they saw the fort. Some of its walls were crumbling, but one tower stood intact, rising about twenty-five feet. The only way to the top of the tower was a narrow set of steps. It was an easily defended stronghold.

With Andreas and Clea helping Prynne, they brought their gear up the stairs. Joe and Clea began preparing backpacks for their hike.

Phil, who was standing lookout, seemed troubled. "How will anyone coming to reinforce us know where we are? That turnoff we took—there's no way we would have found it without Clea's help."

"Ah!" Andreas exclaimed. "I can go back to the place where the road meets and show them."

"What do you mean, 'go back'? You might drive right into the enemy," said Joe.

"Not drive—run!" Andreas said. "I can do that distance in less than one hour."

"And when we raise Salonika on the radio, we can advise any relief force to look for him," Phil added.

"It sounds like our best choice," Prynne mused. "Phil and I will hold down the fort here, while Joe and Clea are—" He stopped abruptly and held up a hand for silence. "We have company."

Phil darted to the wall nearest the road. He called back over his shoulder, "Two cars—ten or more guys with guns getting out of them."

Joe joined Phil. They watched as the group of men fanned out and began to search the area. Prynne positioned himself near the top of the stairs. Shortly afterward a couple of heads peered up at him. Prynne fired two rounds, and the heads vanished.

"Joe!" called Prynne. "How are they armed? Can you tell?"

"I saw more AK-forty-sevens," Joe replied.

"Nothing heavier? No mortars or any kind of artillery?"

"No, just small arms."

Prynne let out a sigh of relief. "Then they can't get up here, and we can't get out. Except we *have* to get you out of here, somehow."

Clea had been exploring the walls. Now she called out, "Joe! Andreas! Over here. I think I've found a way out, if we can keep those men occupied on the other side."

She pointed down the wall, saying, "Do you see the vines here—the way the stones in the wall are uneven? I am sure we have enough footholds and handholds to get down."

Joe surveyed the immediate area, which was almost halfway around the fort from the road. At the foot of the wall, the ground sloped down, but not too steeply. There were scattered boulders, and stunted trees and bushes.

"Once we're down," he said, "it looks as if there's enough cover to let us work our way clear. I think it's our best shot."

Leaving Phil to patrol the wall, Joe outlined the plan. Prynne listened, and when Joe finished, he thought it through for a second.

"It'll have to do," he muttered. "Are you set to move out?"

"Whenever you say," answered Joe, and Clea and Andreas nodded.

Prynne looked at his watch. "In one minute

Phil and I will open up with a heavy covering fire. Give us fifteen seconds to catch the enemy's attention, then make your move. Good luck." Gravely, he shook hands with each of them.

A minute later Prynne and Phil opened up on their side of the fort, firing in frequent, short bursts. The force beneath the walls began firing back. After counting off fifteen seconds, Clea, the most experienced climber, swung herself over the top of the wall.

She made her way carefully, using the tiny crevices between the stones of the wall and the climbing vines. Joe noted the route she took, impressed by her strength and agility, as well as her nerve. He looked over at Andreas.

"Here goes nothing," he said. "See you on the ground floor." Joe swung himself over and began the difficult descent.

Below him Clea had reached a point only three feet from the ground.

But as she dropped, some bushes a few feet from her rustled. Out stepped a man with an old Tokarev pistol—a scout for the attacking party.

And he had Clea dead in his sights!

Chapter

11

THE CELLAR WAS dim, musty, and bare. The men who had kidnapped Frank and the others obviously had faith that they couldn't escape because they removed Peter Stamos's gag and ropes and left his friends unbound. The prisoners were alone now.

As soon as the door had closed, Frank began a quick but thorough search of their dark cell. There was a single, small window, set high into a wall, and protected by a thick steel grill. As a source of light, it was too dirty to be of much use; as a possible escape route it was entirely hopeless.

Moreover, there was nothing—no carelessly dropped tool or removable length of pipe—

nothing that could conceivably serve as a weapon.

Alma huddled, weeping, in a corner, with Aleko hovering over, trying to comfort her.

"What—what will they do to us?" she asked in a shaky, whispery voice.

Aleko knelt before her and put his hands on her shoulders."

"I will not let them hurt you," he said. "They will have to kill me first."

At this, Alma's tears built into sobs that shook her whole body. Chet approached the terrified girl. He bent down and spoke in a calm, casual voice.

"They're not going to do anything to us, Alma. All they want is to keep us out of the way for a while."

She looked up at Chet, wanting to believe him. "Do you think that we are safe?" she asked.

Somehow Chet managed a comforting smile. "Sure, they'll probably hold us until tomorrow and then let us go. Why don't you try to get a little rest?"

She smiled quickly and leaned her head back against the wall, closing her eyes.

For the first time Aleko looked at Chet without hostility. He muttered in gratitude, then began pacing, smacking one massive fist into his other hand with a loud crack.

Moving away from Alma so as not to disturb her, Aleko whispered fiercely, "Frank, I do not know how he could do this."

"Who? Kaliotis?" questioned Frank.

"When we were little, we called him Uncle Nicholas. How could he turn on those who gave him love, gave him *life?* When his parents were killed and his brother taken, he was a small child who would have died if the Stamos family had not taken him in."

He stared at Frank, his burst of anger spent. "I cannot understand it. It is—it is the worst of crimes."

Just then the door at the head of the stairs was flung open, and some men clomped down the steps. Two carried automatic pistols, the third had an Uzi. Fanning out, they trained their guns on the five students.

Then a fourth figure clomped noisily down the wooden steps as everyone watched silently. He surveyed the group with an ugly smirk. And Frank realized that his thin, ferret face was a familiar one—he'd been the ringleader in the attack at the restaurant. Chet gasped and whispered, "Frank! That's the guy from the ship, the one who—"

"You will be silent!" snapped the man in a cold, cutting voice. He looked over to one of the armed men and in the same chilling tone commanded, "Get a brighter light."

"At once, Theo," responded the other, who hastily trotted back up the steps, reappearing a moment later with a long, multicelled flashlight that he handed to Theo.

Theo played the light slowly over the five young faces. Stepping forward, he grasped Frank's collar and jerked him forward a couple of paces.

"Well, well, my meddling young Yankee friend! You have a nasty habit of sticking your nose in where it doesn't belong. I think the time has come for you to pay for your interference."

Frank stared straight into Theo's eyes, refusing to show any fear, concentrating on breathing deeply and evenly.

"Pay?" he said. "Sorry, I didn't think to bring much cash. You take credit cards?"

Switching the flashlight to his left hand, Theo lashed out with his right, catching Frank on the jaw with his open palm and sending him reeling into the wall. Alma gasped, and Chet took a step forward, but stopped when the Uzi was swung around and pointed straight at his chest.

"Enough of this foolishness!" Theo said, slapping the long, heavy flashlight into his palm like a policeman's nightstick. "We have some questions for you." He pointed the flashlight at Frank. "You will answer them immediately and save yourself and your friends unpleasantness."

Frank's jaw hurt, but he would not give Theo the satisfaction of rubbing it and admitting to the pain. "I don't know what kind of information you think you can get out of me. I'm just a student on an exchange program."

"Either you are a fool, which I doubt, or you take me for one." Theo leaned in until his face was inches from Frank's. "I want to know exactly where your criminal accomplices are to meet with the American spy. He will not escape the forces of justice in any case, but if you tell us the exact location of the meeting, it will be easier for him—and for you."

Frank took a deep breath, but let none of the relief and happiness he felt show in his face. Maybe Joe and the rest of the northern party had somehow managed to get free of the ambush.

"Spy? Criminal accomplices? Listen, Theo, I'm telling you, you're making a mistake. We came here to study history and culture.

"I tell you what, check with my brother Joe. He'll be happy to explain how we've always wanted to visit Greece and soak up all this ancient history."

"I look forward to the chance of having a long, long meeting with your brother, when such a thing is possible. But for now," Theo said, "I am talking to *you*. So, stop this pointless lying. Where is this meeting to be?"

Frank shrugged and shook his head. "Sorry, but I'm afraid I can't help you."

Theo's eyes narrowed, and his lips pressed together into a thin, bloodless line. He handed the flashlight to one of his henchmen and reached into his jacket, pulling out a large, nickel-plated 9mm automatic pistol. Holding it casually at the bridge of Frank's nose, he asked, "Perhaps this will help your memory a little?"

To Frank, the barrel of the gun looked about the size of a manhole cover. But he gave Theo his most innocent, puzzled look and replied, "There's nothing I can tell you. And if you shoot me, then there definitely will be nothing I'll be able to tell you."

"Shoot *you?* Oh, no, my young student friend, I would never dream of shooting *you*." Theo's mouth curved up into a smile, and that smile was the ugliest expression he had shown yet—the look of a shark that had just sniffed out a tasty meal.

"No, *you* are to remain alive for the time being," Theo went on. "But I am going to introduce your friends here to a very old custom of our country—one which your brother and you, with your great interest in Greek history, will no doubt find fascinating."

Theo put his gun away and climbed the steps out of the cellar, returning a moment later with a small clay pot in his hand. "It is a kind of lottery," he explained.

Pulling a knife from a sheath on his belt, Theo crossed the basement. The wall there had once been decorated with black and white tiles. Many were now missing or broken. Theo pried several of the tiles loose, then slipped the knife back in its sheath.

"You see," Theo said, holding the tiles out in his hand, "I have three white tiles and one black one. When the ancients had to choose one person from a group to suffer an unpleasant fate, they put tiles or rocks in a pot, like so."

He dropped the tiles into the pot and shook it up. "Then each member of the group would pick a tile. The person with the bad luck to draw the black tile—that one would suffer. Now we relive this old Greek custom. Fun, eh?"

Frank reached for the pot, but Theo shook his head.

"Oh, no, my friend, you may only observe our little lottery," Theo said. "But the rest of you"—he swung his gaze over Chet, Peter, Alma, and Aleko—"will reach into the pot and choose a tile. Whoever chooses the black tile, that unhappy soul will suffer if Frank refuses to answer my questions.''

He smiled again. ''Whether you live or die will be entirely Frank's responsibility.''

Chapter

12

JOE HARDY CLUNG to the rocky surface of the old fortress tower like a fly to sticky paper. He was only halfway down when the gunman had appeared to subdue Clea.

Apparently the enemy scout had seen only her and decided on a quiet capture. He had clamped a hand over her mouth and begun dragging her backward.

But Clea refused to cooperate. She sank her teeth into the guy's hand. He grunted in pain and lost his grip on the girl, who darted away. He recovered quickly and lunged after her.

Twelve feet above, Joe pushed out from the wall. Falling like dead weight, he hit his unsuspecting target squarely on the back. They both fell heavily, with the man taking most of the impact.

Joe kicked free and got to his feet, while his dazed opponent wobbled to his hands and knees. Before he got up any farther, Joe delivered a roundhouse right to the side of the guy's head with enough power to send him flat on his face, down and out.

Clea rushed up as Joe removed the unconscious gunman's pistol and checked the clip. There was a full load of eight shots. He made sure the safety was on and stuck the gun in his belt.

"Are you all right?" Clea asked.

"Never felt better," he answered, pulling a coil of rope from his pack. "Let's drag him over behind the bushes there and tie him up."

They left the scout behind a dense growth of plants, a gag stuffed in his mouth and his hands and feet bound behind his back. By this time, Andreas had joined them. They still heard occasional firing from the other side of the tower.

"Okay," Joe said. "Clea and I will circle in front of the tower and create a diversion with this." He patted the pistol.

"I figure if they think they're under fire from two sides, that ought to let Andreas move down the hillside without being seen. Andreas, you have a watch?"

"A stopwatch for my running," he replied, pulling one from a pocket.

"Great!" exclaimed Joe. "Give us, say, ten minutes from the time we move out before you take off. And one last thing—when you get to that junction, stay out of sight until you're sure that the people you see are *friendly*. Got that?"

Andreas's eyes gleamed with excitement. "I understand," he assured Joe. Then he smiled at his sister. "Take care, and good luck."

Clea gave Andreas a quick hug. "Run well, my brother."

Leaving Andreas looking at his watch, Joe and Clea worked their way down the slope. They carefully started around the fortress, using all available cover once they were within sight of the attack force.

Dodging from scraggly bush to little hillock of earth, to one of the many boulders scattered around the area, they moved in behind the enemy. They climbed a hill, at their opponents' backs. The gunmen never noticed a thing.

"Over here," Joe whispered. He'd seen just what he wanted—a thick tangle of bushes on the hill's crest. From there they could see a section of road where Andreas should soon appear. The nearest of the opposition was about sixty yards away. Joe checked his watch and found that eight minutes had passed. They had two minutes to establish their diversion.

Joe motioned Clea to lie flat and pulled out the automatic pistol, flipping off the safety. He drew a bead on the rock the nearest enemy was using for cover. Then, gripping the heavy pistol in two hands, as his father had taught him, he squeezed off a shot.

Sixty yards away, the bullet smashed into a rock only a foot from the gunman, who jumped in fear and stared wildly around. Joe fired again, and a bullet ricocheted off a rock on the man's *other* side, sending up a shower of stone chips.

Joe and Clea could hear the man cry out in shrill, panicky tones. Joe kept shooting until the clip was empty. The result was a frantic scramble as the bewildered attackers looked for better hiding places against gunfire from both the tower and this new threat. A burst of wild automatic fire tore through the top of a tree, but the gunner had no idea where to aim.

Clea reached out to tap Joe on the arm. "Look! On the road!" she whispered urgently.

Joe swung around and saw Andreas, arms churning, thin legs pumping, as he sprinted away, completely unseen by the enemy. The diversion had worked!

Seconds later heavy fire erupted from the tower, and the attackers, now totally rattled, turned back to face their original target.

Joe nudged Clea. "I think Phil and Prynne

are giving us some cover. Let's take advantage of it and get out of here. Stay low and move slowly—at first."

They put some distance between the fortress and themselves before they felt it was safe to take off across the jagged terrain at a rapid clip. The noise of shooting soon faded behind them.

They moved through a landscape of barren earth and stone. Drab, colorless, low trees and bushes were the only silhouettes breaking up the monotony. There were no buildings, no signs of paved roads, in fact, no evidence that people had ever set foot there. Clea had some knowledge of the country and led the way. At one point, Joe called a brief halt and discarded their pistol, hiding it under a pile of small rocks.

Clea asked, "Why don't we keep the gun?"

"If we're stopped by anyone," answered Joe, "it's better if we look like a couple of innocent backpackers. And an empty pistol isn't going to be of much use anyway."

They plodded on for a while in silence, each wrapped up in his or her own thoughts and worries about friends and relations.

Joe began to be aware of the straps of his pack cutting into his shoulders. And his legs were sending painful messages that all this up- and downhill was getting very old very fast.

He stopped and drew in a deep breath. "Listen, Clea." She turned to face him. "Uh, how are you doing? You want to take a breather?"

"A breather?" she asked with a mocking smile. "Can it be that the all-American athlete is tired already?"

Joe felt his face reddening. "Hey, give me a break!" he protested. "I'm fine, I just figured maybe you might be a little—"

"You needn't worry about *me*," replied Clea coldly. "Any Greek could outlast you in cross-country hiking. I see how the American tourists won't go anywhere if they can't take a bus or car. You're soft and weak, all of you."

Joe's aching legs and back were forgotten in a rising tide of anger and resentment. He marched alongside her, demanding, "Why do you hate America anyway? What's your problem?"

Clea stared at him in puzzlement. "Hate America? I don't. We Greeks owe a great deal to your country. America saved us from terrible things when my parents were young."

Joe frowned. "I don't get it."

"After World War Two ended, there were those who wanted Greece to become a Communist state. Many died in the fighting, and thousands of children, babies even, were carried off to be raised in Communist countries.

97

When we became a tyranny, they would return as our new leaders.

"If it had not been for American assistance, the Communists might have won. But when I see rich, spoiled American tourists who only want their comforts, I wonder if they could fight for their liberty if they had to."

Joe had forgotten his anger as he listened to Clea's story. He walked a way before answering.

"I never heard any of what happened in Greece back then," he said finally. "I'm glad you told me. But I do know a bit about America. Sure, there are some folks like the ones you're talking about, who come over for a good time only.

"But I look at Bayport, where Frank and I live, and people don't look so lazy or spoiled to me. They work hard. My father, for instance, makes a good, comfortable living as a detective, but I can tell you, he's worked hard to help a lot of people."

He looked down. "I guess that's one of the reasons my brother and I want to be like him."

Clea shook her head. "What you say may be true, but that's just one town and only a small number of people."

"Frank and I have met a lot of Americans. I'm not saying they're all perfect, but I don't think we're all that bad. In fact, I bet we're a lot like you. We look at some things differently, we do some stuff differently. But I guess we're the same in more important ways than we're different.''

Joe broke off, seeing Clea smile at him. He looked away, embarrassed at having gone on as he had.

"Well, anyway, that's what I think," he mumbled. "Maybe it sounds pretty dumb, but—"

"No, not at all," Clea protested. "I don't think it's dumb at all, Joe. I think that it is probably so. Perhaps I do not know Americans as well as I thought I did. Maybe we're both learning important things from each other."

They went on in silence again—a friendlier silence than before.

Near the crest of what seemed to Joe like the two hundredth hill they'd climbed, he raised his hands in mock surrender and said, "Okay, I give up. *I* want to take a breather, because *I* could use a break, all right?"

Clea began to pull off her backpack. "If you hadn't said anything, I would have in a minute or so," she admitted. "I think we could both use a little rest and something to eat."

Joe noticed a flat ledge of rock nearby. He walked over to it, shedding his own pack as he did. "This looks like a pretty good spot to sit down for a couple of—"

Whap! Something smacked into the pack, ripping it out of his hands. Startled, Joe yelled to Clea, "Get down!"

She stared in surprise but dove for the ground.

Crouching, Joe scanned the barren hillsides around them. Somewhere out there, someone had targeted them. But there'd been no sound of a gunshot.

"We've got to get behind those rocks," he said to Clea, glancing at the only cover nearby.

Joe and the Greek girl managed to crawl only a foot toward shelter.

Then something went *spang* off the rocks right between them.

Chapter

13

THEO SHOVED THE small pot with the four tiles inside at Chet Morton, saying, "We'll begin with you, fat boy. Put your hand inside and pick out a tile. Quickly!"

Glaring at the man, jaws clenched tight, Chet reached in and pulled out a tile. It sat in his large fist as he swallowed, then opened his hand. The tile was white!

Theo was clearly enjoying the game and the fear it caused his prisoners. He moved over to Aleko, who scowled sullenly. "Now you, make your choice. Don't be afraid, boy, the odds are still in your favor."

"I am not afraid," muttered Aleko as he pulled out a tile. It, too, was white.

"It is the turn of the young lady," Theo said, offering her the pot. Alma stared at him, eyes wide, frozen, like a bird hypnotized by a snake. She couldn't move.

"Come, now," Theo went on, shaking the pot so that the two remaining tiles rattled. "Get it done with, girl. You are making me angry, and that is a very bad idea. *Take the tile,* or I will make your brother my first victim!"

"No! Please!" cried Alma, groping inside the pot with a trembling hand. Looking at what she had chosen, she let out a soft moaning sound. Her hand fell to her side, and the black tile dropped to the cellar floor.

Theo grabbed Alma by the wrist. He pulled her forward, away from the others, drawing the big automatic with his other hand.

"Let her go," roared Aleko, springing for Theo's throat. The henchman with the long flashlight clubbed the brawny young Greek on the back of the head, dropping him in a crumpled heap on the ground. Alma screamed, but Theo silenced her abruptly, pointing the ugly gun at her nostrils. The room grew quiet.

"Now then! There will be no more heroics, I hope," Theo said, looking over at Frank.

"If you wish this girl to live, you will tell me all you know about where the meeting has been set with the criminal spy—now!"

Frank gauged the distance that separated

him from Theo—but with three other armed men facing him, the odds were too long. Theo held Alma by the wrist, and now, deliberately, he cocked his gun with a dry click that echoed through the room. Then the door at the head of the steps opened.

"Theo!" called out a voice, and Nicholas Kaliotis stormed the cellar. Theo sullenly lowered his weapon. The two men shouted angrily at each other in Greek. Kaliotis turned to Frank, giving him a grim look.

"We do not wish to hurt anyone. You will all be released unharmed, if you are cooperative."

"Traitor!" Alma shrieked. "How can anything you say be believed?"

Kaliotis bit his lower lip but did not look at her.

"I tell you, we are not here to shed blood. You must tell us what you know, and you and your friends will be safe. I swear it."

Frank studied Kaliotis for a few seconds. "Maybe you actually believe what you're saying," he answered. "I wish that *I* could. We've seen too much, we know too much, and your buddy Theo seems like a guy who would shoot because he doesn't like the way we cut our hair. I don't think it matters if I say anything or not."

"No! You are wrong, I tell you!" Kaliotis

grabbed Frank's shoulders with both hands. "I would not have done this—do you think I would have brought you here to be *shot?*"

Theo stepped forward between Kaliotis and Frank and shoved the Greek back and out of the way. He gave Kaliotis a look of contempt.

"We have tried your method, and you see where it has gotten us. Now we are short of time, and we will use *my* way. I will shoot a prisoner now, and one for each additional minute that this stubborn American refuses to talk."

Kaliotis started to protest, but Theo grabbed Alma once again, saying, "You are weak, my brother."

He aimed the pistol at Alma, and once more looked over at Frank. "Well? What will it be? Nothing? Very well, then. Her death is on your head, Yankee."

"Theo! No!" Just before Theo pulled the trigger, Kaliotis hurled himself at Theo. The pistol roared, and Kaliotis was flung back against the wall.

Seeing his chance, Frank drove a shoulder hard into Theo's chest, knocking him down and sending the gun clattering into a corner. Chet wrenched the flashlight away from the distracted guard and brought it down on the man's arm as he raised *his* pistol. Then he rammed an elbow into the face of the disarmed gunman, who fell to his knees, all the fight knocked out of him.

Screaming, Alma rushed the man with the Uzi, clawing at his eyes. Peter jumped on the guy's back, pinning the man's arms to his sides, hanging in with grim determination. The man, bleeding from the scratches that Alma had left on his face, tried to shake Peter loose, but the boy wouldn't let go.

The remaining guard leveled his pistol, hoping for a clear shot at one of the young demons. But in the dim light the action boiled so rapidly around him that he dared not shoot.

While he hesitated, Chet threw the long multicell flashlight at him. It struck him a glancing blow that didn't do much damage. But it was followed immediately by Chet himself, who slammed the guard against the wall of the cellar and knocked the wind out of him.

Theo was tough and agile, quickly getting up and going for the gun lying in the corner. When Frank tried to hook an arm around his leg, he kicked back, landing a heel on Frank's forehead hard enough to leave him briefly stunned.

Now Theo had eyes only for his gun—*he* wouldn't hesitate to shoot the wrong person. But as he strode toward the gleaming automatic, a hand reached out to trip him up. Aleko, only partially conscious, was still in the fight. Theo landed hard, the gun a few feet beyond his outstretched hand.

Snarling in frustration, Theo jerked his foot loose from Aleko's grip and kicked back with his heavy boot on Aleko's arm. Then he started to crawl forward but stopped short and sagged in defeat. Frank Hardy, bleeding slightly from a cut on his forehead, stood with the silvery pistol in his hand. He fired a single shot, which split the air with an ear-shattering roar. A moment later all the guns had been collected by Peter and Chet. Alma knelt beside her brother as he started to come around.

Nicholas Kaliotis lay motionless, the sleeve and body of his shirt marked by a spreading stain of red. Frank started over to him. "Mr. Kaliotis? Nicholas?"

When Peter and Chet also turned to Nicholas, Theo saw his opportunity. With a single lithe movement, he was on his feet, and before anyone could react, he had an iron grip around Alma's neck, and a knife at her throat. Furious at his own carelessness, Frank trained his gun on Theo, who sneered, pulling Alma back toward the foot of the stairs.

"No, no, young American, don't be hasty. I am going to take my leave of you now—but I am certain that we'll be seeing each other again, quite soon."

Keeping his eyes fixed on the guns held by

Frank, Chet and Peter, Theo climbed the steep flight of stairs, pulling Alma up step by step, using her as a shield. When he reached the top landing, he held the knife against Alma, and reached back with his other hand to push open the door. With one last malevolent stare at Frank, Theo vanished through the doorway, leaving Alma standing alone and trembling.

"C'mon, Frank, let's get him," urged Chet.

But Frank let his gun hand drop to his side. "No, we'd never catch him—he knows this city, and we don't. Besides, we have some people who need looking after. He'll keep, for the moment. Alma, are you okay?"

Alma had her arms crossed, hugging herself tightly. She took a ragged breath and said, "Yes, I think so. I am not hurt, only . . . I was very frightened. But I am well." She started back down the steps.

Peter was kneeling by Kaliotis. "Frank! He's alive. His eyes are open, and I think he's conscious."

Frank got down next to Kaliotis, who looked up with a mixture of pain and remorse. The man panted with effort. In spite of his shoulder wound, he reached out with his other hand to grip Frank's arm. "You must believe that I never thought he would shoot. I was wrong, and you were right."

Frank gently removed Kaliotis's hand and

spoke quietly. "Just try to relax, and we'll get some help for you."

Kaliotis nodded weakly. "I am not seriously wounded, I think. No immediate danger."

"Mr. Kaliotis—Nicholas," Frank went on. "Theo called you 'brother' a while back. Why did he do that?"

Kaliotis's eyes closed, and he sighed. "He *is* my brother by birth—he was taken across the border many years before. Some months ago, he revealed his identity to me, telling me things about our family that only my brother could possibly know."

A bitter look came over the man's face. "He said that things had changed since the civil war, that he was fighting for a just cause, and that he would permit no killing. I wanted to believe. But now . . ." His face hardened. "We may have had the same mother, but we are brothers no longer."

"Don't talk any more," Frank said as Chet came up with an old blanket he had found to cover the wounded man. "Just take it easy, and help will be here in a little while." Frank stood up, and looked over to where Alma was tending Aleko. The muscular young Greek was sitting with his back against a wall, fully awake and alert.

Frank surveyed him a moment. "How are you making out?"

Aleko managed a faint grin. "My head—it hurts very bad. But I will be all right. I—*we* owe you much."

Frank waved a hand. "Hey, we all did our bit. You, too, for that matter. But we still have a lot to do. Peter and Alma, you had better stay here with Nicholas and Aleko. Chet, let's get moving."

"First thing," Frank continued, "we find a phone and let Spiros Stamos know what's happened—that we've found Peter, and that Kaliotis needs a doctor. Then we try to make radio contact with Joe and the others up north."

He looked grim. "With Theo on the loose, we're likely to find a hot time on the border—all too soon."

Chapter

14

JOE LAY FROZEN in the open, thinking that if there was anything worse than being shot at, it was not knowing where the shots were coming from. He waited to see what would happen next. If people were sniping at them, he and Clea couldn't try anything until they showed themselves.

From the cover of a gnarled and stunted tree trunk thirty feet away, a boy stepped forward. The kid couldn't have been more than thirteen or fourteen. He wore a ragged T-shirt, old jeans belted with a piece of rope, and sandals on his feet. He was carrying a long piece of rawhide. He glared at the two strangers.

Clea spoke to Joe in a whisper, never taking

her eyes off the boy. "He is a shepherd, and he shot at you with that sling he is holding."

As she spoke, the boy pulled a smooth stone a bit larger than a marble from a pouch hanging from his rope belt and fitted it into the sling. He addressed them in Greek, sounding angry to Joe. Clea replied, and there was a short conversation between the two. Joe heard a familiar word—*Amerikanos*—Greek for American.

The boys eyes widened. *"Amerikanos?"* he echoed softly, dropping the stone back into the pouch and letting the sling fall. He was transformed, now carrying on with a stream of friendly chatter.

"He is called Giannis," Clea translated. "He says that border guards have been coming from Yugoslavia and raiding his flock, taking his sheep for food. He has been making patrols lately and moves his flock frequently."

There was another interval of talk between Clea and Giannis in Greek, and Clea turned to Joe in some excitement. "He knows the cabin we are looking for! It is no more than a fifteen minute walk from this spot."

Clea resumed her talk with the shepherd, who spoke for a longer time, with Clea listening and nodding her head in agreement. She explained to Joe: "It will not be hard to find—it is just over that hill, there." She pointed to a gentle slope about half a mile away. "But he warns us that we must be very careful and watch for the border patrols. He says the guards are the kind who shoot first and ask questions later, if at all."

Joe smiled at the boy, saying to Clea, "Be sure to thank him for me."

Clea spoke to Giannis, and the boy looked down shyly, then stepped closer to Joe, saying something directly to him for the first time. Joe looked questioningly at Clea, who tried to hide a grin.

"Giannis said that, since you are from America, perhaps you know his uncle George, who lives in America in a town called Chicago."

Joe looked at the shepherd, who stared at him hopefully, and shook his head.

"Uncle George drives a taxicab," Clea added.

"Tell him I'm sorry, but I've never met Uncle George," Joe said, keeping his face serious as he did so. "But if I ever do run into him, I will tell him that his nephew Giannis was very helpful to me."

When Clea relayed this speech, Giannis glowed with pride. Opening their packs, they took out food and offered some to Giannis. The young shepherd hesitated, and then took what was offered, wolfing it down as if he hadn't eaten in days. Joe and Clea finished their meal, thanked the boy once more, and headed off toward the last hill and the cabin beyond.

As they hiked, Joe looked back once more at Giannis, who stood watching them. "He seems kind of young to be out here by himself."

"He is not so young that he cannot help his family make their living," Clea answered. "People in the mountains are very poor. They can't afford to be children for very long."

They climbed the hill that Giannis had pointed out to them and began to descend the far side. Partway down, they caught sight of a small tumbledown hut standing by itself near the foot of the hill. Joe stared at it. "Calling that a cabin gives it the benefit of the doubt. If you ask me, I'd call it a shack."

The place seemed to be deserted. They waited for a few minutes; there was no sign of activity.

Joe slipped out of his pack and handed it to Clea. "I'm going down to check it out. You stay here." He scrambled down the slope till he reached the cabin. He peered in through a hole in the wall, then came to a crude door. It swung open with a loud creak.

Inside the dim light was alive with dust motes. A very old mattress lay along one wall and a three-legged table was on its side nearby. Otherwise the room was empty.

Joe climbed back up to Clea and squatted down near her. "All clear. We're the first to arrive, and I think we should stay up here, where we have a view of anyone coming. Let's get comfortable—we might be a while."

They found good cover and settled in to wait. Joe was half-asleep in the late-afternoon sun when Clea poked him with her foot. "I think someone is coming."

Joe stared where Clea was pointing. A man was indeed heading toward the cabin from the north. He was plainly straining, pushing on despite the fatigue that made his stride a little wobbly. From time to time he paused to look behind him.

As the man neared the cabin, Joe and Clea began to pick their way toward him. They walked through a patch of gravel, and the man spun to face them.

Clearly, they weren't what he was expecting. He tried speaking to them, first in a language that neither Joe nor Clea knew, then in Greek.

Joe now took a few steps toward the man, who was obviously on his last legs. The agent hadn't shaved in days. His eyes were red rimmed and glazed; only willpower was keeping him on his feet. He took another quick glance back in the direction from which he'd come.

Finally Joe decided that he had to be their contact. "It's all right. You must be Atlas. We're, uh, friends of Mr. Prynne—I think you know him as Ajax—anyway, he couldn't be here himself because of an accident, and—well, it's a long story. So here we are instead, okay?"

The man stared and shook his head slowly. "I can't believe it. You're just a couple of kids."

Joe straightened up and said, "Well, I'm seventeen, and so's Clea here, if that's what you mean. Sorry, I tried to get older, but this is the best I could do."

The man squatted down, staring up at Joe and Clea, raking his hair back with his fingers. "You two have any weapons?"

"Afraid not," Joe answered. "Sorry."

"You wouldn't, by any chance, have something to eat and drink? It's been quite a while since I had any food."

Joe stripped off his pack and found him some bread and cheese. The man tore at the bread and stuffed hunks of cheese into his mouth. Clea wordlessly gave him her canteen, and he took several long swallows.

"Can't tell you how much I needed that," he said once the little meal was done. "Wish I had time for an after-dinner nap, but we'd better get moving. We're going to have company any minute now. We are on the Greek side of the border, aren't we?''

"Yes, you are in Greece," Clea said. "The line is just north of that cabin.''

The man slowly got to his feet and stretched. "We'd better head out of here anyway. With what I'm carrying, the people on my tail aren't about to let a little thing like a national border get in their way. You two kids actually work for . . . I mean, I knew they'd been having some recruiting problems, but . . .''

Joe shrugged back into his pack. "We're not exactly Network operatives, if that's what you're getting at. We sort of fell into this job. Things haven't been going according to plan, but it doesn't sound like we have time for a long story just now. Shall we get going?''

"Lead on. By the way, what do I call you two?''

"She's Clea and I'm Joe. Joe Hardy.''

"Pleased to meet you. I wish it had been under different circumstances." Clea took the lead as they began to retrace their steps back toward the south. As they climbed the hill, agent Atlas kept looking behind them, as he strained to keep up the pace. Joe observed Atlas's concern. "Who are you expecting to follow us?''

"There was a Yugoslav patrol about ten miles back. I managed to give them the slip and must have built up a little lead. But I know they're back there somewhere.

Joe peered into the distance, but saw no signs of movement. They returned to their hurried climb. As they neared the top, Atlas no longer kept glancing back. He seemed to be rapidly running out of energy: his breathing had become more labored, and he was limping slightly as if there were a rock in one of his shoes.

"You okay?" Joe asked him.

"Don't bother worrying about me. How far do we have to go, and do you have any friends waiting when we get there?"

"It's between an hour and a half and two hours, and there's at least a few friends there—with guns. Maybe more of them by now."

"Very good," said Atlas. "Okay, Joe, you and Clea don't have to worry about me. I'll do what I have to, to get back home. I'd just feel better if we had a weapon, but—"

Crack! The unmistakable sound of a high-powered rifle rang out, and a puff of dust and dirt spouted a few feet to Joe's right side.

"There they are," said Atlas, pointing north. Joe quickly counted about a dozen men in tan uniforms, all armed, jogging down the slope of the next hill over, perhaps three hundred yards behind them. More shots were fired, and a ricochet whined off a nearby rock.

The sight of the pursuers seemed to destroy Atlas's energy. His shoulders slumped, and he reeled as if someone had hit him.

"Let's go!" snapped Joe. "Let's stay about ten yards apart and take advantage of all the cover you can find—at least till we're over the crest of the hill. Move!"

As they clambered up their hill, Joe risked another look back. The border guards had formed a ragged line, picking up speed as they came. They had their target in sight, and they'd guessed right that the target couldn't shoot back. A few of them had even broken into a full run.

The hunters were closing in rapidly—and there wasn't a thing that Joe, Clea, or Atlas could do to stop them.

Chapter

15

A CAR SPED north along the same road that Joe, Prynne, Clea, and the others had taken earlier. At the wheel was Spiros Stamos, with Frank Hardy next to him, the multiband radio in his lap. In the backseat were the Gray Man and Chet Morton.

After Frank and Chet had left the cellar where they'd been held captive, things had come together in a hurry. Medical attention had been provided for Nicholas Kaliotis and for Aleko, both of whom would recover.

In the case of Kaliotis, there were legal matters to be dealt with once he left the hospital, and he was in police custody. But he was willing, even eager, to help bring Theo and his thugs to justice.

Earlier, when Frank had gotten in the car, he exclaimed, "This is the big rescue force you talked about? The four of us? What's the deal here, is the Network running on a supertight budget or something?"

The Gray Man had replied, "Take it easy, Frank. The Greek military can't get involved in this, and neither can any other official arm of the Greek government, unless we want serious diplomatic problems. It can't seem that they took any official interest in this matter at all. And there *is* a larger party, which will come after us. We're just the vanguard, so to speak."

Now they were twisting and turning along the mountain roads, carefully taking the switchbacks and hairpins. Frank fiddled with the radio, but he didn't hear anything except static. He was feeling edgy and tried not to let it show. There hadn't been any information about Joe and the others for hours.

Abruptly, Stamos braked the car to a stop and backed it up. Half-hidden in a cleft between some rocks stood an all-terrain vehicle.

"That must be the ATV Prynne was driving this morning," he said.

They pulled in next to the truck and behind it found a group of men, tied up. The bound men wouldn't speak, but the Gray Man noticed a piece of paper pinned on one guy's shirt. He reached down and pulled it loose.

"Somebody's left a note. 'To whom it may concern,' " the Gray Man read. " 'We had to borrow a car from these guys after they shot up our truck. We're on our way north. See you soon—we hope. Joe.' "

After Spiro Stamos radioed in to arrange for the prisoners to be picked up, they headed back out on the road. Frank took control of the radio, switching it to the proper frequency. Before he had a chance to try a transmission, the voice of Phil Cohen crackled out of the speaker. Eagerly, Frank grabbed the microphone.

"Phil! This is Frank, Phil! Do you read me? Do you read me? Over?"

Phil's response was audible through a slight filter of static and interference. "Affirmative, Frank, you're coming through pretty well. Good to hear a friendly voice over this thing!"

"What's happening with you up there? We're on our way to join you. Over."

"It's kind of involved, so I'll try to keep it simple. We drove the Mercedes we took from that bunch of heavies, but we decided to turn off from the main route and take a side road that goes right by this old Turkish fort. Prynne got hurt when we took the car, by the way— messed up his leg, so he can't walk."

The radio hissed and popped with static for a second, then Phil's voice came through again. "He and I are holed up on top of the fort's tower, and there're maybe five guys with small arms down below. We can hold 'em off as long as our ammo holds out, because they haven't got anything heavy enough to knock the tower down."

Frank cut in on Phil. "How's Joe? Is he with you? Over."

"Joe and Clea have gone out to make the meeting at the border and bring Atlas back. So it's just me and Prynne here right now, but that'll be enough—till our ammunition runs down. Over."

Spiros Stamos took the mike from Frank. "Listen, Phil—you say you took another road, off the main route. How will we know where that road is? Is there any kind of sign or landmark? Over."

"We sent Andreas down from here on foot, to point out where you turn. He should be there now. Keep an eye out for him. Over."

Frank took the mike back. "I copy that," he said. "We just passed your ATV and the bunch you left tied up there."

"Then you'll get to the road junction in less than half an hour." Suddenly the volume of static rose, and Phil's voice faded. Frank turned his volume control as high as it would go and strained his ears, but all he could make out was "See you . . . hurry . . . luck . . ." Then the noise took over completely.

Frank stared in frustration at the radio and flicked the set off. The Gray Man leaned forward over the front seat. "Radio contact is tough when you're going through the mountains. But it sounds like they're doing well."

Frank wasn't about to get his hopes up too easily. "Yeah, they're doing all right—unless they run out of ammo, or heavier guns show up for the bad guys. And we don't know what's happening with Joe and Clea. Can't we get any more speed out of this thing?"

"The idea is to arrive there in one piece." Spiros Stamos didn't take his eyes off the road as the car lurched along a roller coaster-like dip, followed by a tight turn. "We cannot help anyone if we wind up in the bottom of that ravine beside us."

Stamos's knuckles were white as he took the car through another hairpin, bringing the right front wheel within less than a foot of the drop. "Be patient, Frank. To go faster in this area is crazy—suicide."

Frank forced himself to be cool and let Stamos do the driving. He stared silently out at the drab countryside flying by. But he could restrain himself for only so long, as grim thoughts about Joe kept popping up in his mind. He turned back to look at Stamos.

"Maybe I ought to drive for a while. You could probably use a break."

Stamos continued to stare straight ahead. "I know you are worried about your brother, Frank. But do not forget—my son and daughter are there as well, facing the same dangers. We will do all that can be done, but we must not let our worries make us try foolish things."

Frank settled back in his seat, feeling a little ashamed. He *had* forgotten that he wasn't the only one in the car with a strong personal interest in getting safely and quickly where they were going.

Frank suddenly sat bolt upright, focusing his eyes farther down the road. Had he actually seen something flashing by the roadside, or was he imagining— No! There it was again, a glint of metal from the bushes—a signal, maybe?

"Mr. Stamos," Frank began, "do you see a bright—" and he broke off. From the clump of brush where the flashes had come, he could just make out something moving. It was an arm! Someone was hiding there, pointing upward. Why?

Frank looked up, trying to figure out what the unseen figure was pointing to.

The hillside rose steeply, though it wasn't

sheer cliff at this spot. Frank's gaze moved up, then he shouted, "Stop! Look out! Up there, on our left!"

Bouncing down the hill like a giant, misshapen bowling ball, a huge boulder was crashing its way toward the road.

And it was headed right for their car!

Chapter
16

CLEA, JOE, AND ATLAS cleared the top of the hill and plunged down the slope on the other side. They were able to put some more distance between themselves and their hunters, but only for a while. The border guards knew their quarry would run and not fight. The gap had to close again and quickly.

Atlas hadn't complained, but he was clearly in no shape for a long running chase. He had reached the outer limits of his endurance. But they had no choice other than to keep moving, heading south.

Behind them, the faster, more ambitious guards raced ahead of their comrades. Joe could hear them calling to one another.

One guard in particular had a sizable lead over the others. He cleared the top of the rise and broke into a near-sprint, ignoring the shouts of the others who couldn't match his pace. This target would be his, and his alone!

Running grimly ahead, he closed the distance. A hundred yards between them— eighty—sixty . . . Now the man they had been chasing for so long had begun to lag behind. The spy was running awkwardly, only twenty yards ahead. He looked back over his shoulder, saw the patrol guard coming, and turned to face him.

The guard knelt down, propping his AK-47 on a flat rock to steady it. Then he drew a careful bead on his prey.

Up ahead, Joe looked back to see the guard aiming at Atlas. There was no cover for the American, and the guard was too close to miss.

Then the guard flung a hand up over his face and slumped sideways, his gun rattling on the rock. He lay motionless. Joe saw Atlas dart forward toward the mysteriously fallen gunman, when he realized that a voice was whispering to him from some nearby undergrowth.

"*Amerikanos!* Hey *Amerikanos!*" Branches parted, and a thin, young face appeared between them. It was Giannis! The young shepherd waved his sling and made frantic beckoning gestures. Joe waved back in agreement, turning to locate Clea, who was staring in surprise at the downed guard.

"Clea! This way! Come on, move it!" She scrambled toward him. Atlas, Joe noted, had now grabbed the guard's gun and ammunition, and was starting back downhill. Soon all three were lying behind the concealing undergrowth along with Giannis.

Clea introduced Atlas to the shepherd, and Atlas admired Giannis's sling. "You tell him he's quite a marksman with that thing. He saved my bacon just now."

Clea passed on the compliment to Giannis, who grinned broadly.

Atlas was checking out the captured automatic weapon. "I think we may be able to slow our friends down some, if this young fellow with the sling will help us out some more."

Clea translated the request, and Giannis replied eagerly.

"He says that he's happy to help. Maybe they will think twice before stealing a lamb for their dinner."

Atlas knelt down facing the others.

"Okay. These clowns out there think we're unarmed and helpless. Now, one gun and a little ammo isn't much good in a real fight, but it'll be fine for *show*." He looked like a new man with a weapon in his hands.

"Suppose you two head on down to the foot

of the hill and find cover. Clea, you tell Giannis that I'm going to fire a few bursts at those guards when they get closer. When I do that, I want him to plink another one of those sheep-rustlers for me. Just put one of them out of action.

"Once they realize that we *do* have guns, that'll slow them down. They won't know that it's just the one weapon. Also, they can't afford to leave their wounded here, on the wrong side of the border where the Greek police might find them. So they'll have to detail men to stay with the injured guys, to make sure they get back home.

"Then I'll join you two at the bottom of the hill. Tell Giannis to stay buttoned up here until the guards have gone by, then hightail it out of here. He'd better move his flock away for a while, too."

After shaking hands with Giannis, Joe and Clea started down the hillside again, keeping the bushes between themselves and the border guards as much as possible. A few scattered shots were fired, but the patrol members were out of effective range.

Joe turned back when he heard the burst from Atlas's AK-47. He saw a man sprawl forward on the ground, while his comrades scattered, looking for cover from the unexpected gunfire.

"Giannis strikes again," remarked Joe to Clea. "Let's find a place to wait for Atlas."

Presently Atlas came limping down to the bottom of the slope, glancing back toward the pursuers. "They seem to have gotten our message. There are only seven or eight following us—and they're likely to keep a respectful distance. We ought to be able to mount a pretty good rear-guard action and get back to your buddies in the tower."

They set off, at a less frantic pace than before. The border patrol seemed content just to shadow them.

After a while Joe tapped Clea on the arm. "I figure we should be getting close to the fortress by now. See any familiar landmarks?"

Clea studied the area. "We ought to be very—listen!" The breeze brought the sound of shooting, coming from not too far ahead of them.

"We're back," said Joe, "and they're still holding on at the tower."

Atlas was making his way in their direction, looking back over his shoulder periodically. Joe ran out to meet him.

"The fortress is just a little bit ahead and to our right," Joe reported. "We heard some firing from that direction."

"Great. Let's get someplace where we can see how it lays. If we can surprise the guys attacking the tower, maybe we can break through before they know what's going on.''

In front of them the ground sloped gently, but to their right it became steeper. From the echoing gunfire, the fight was going on just on the other side of that hill.

"Let's get ourselves to the top, and see what we can," Atlas said. They began to climb, slowly and cautiously, not knowing how close they were to the action beyond. At the summit, they looked down into a little valley, beyond which was a somewhat higher hill. "I guess that's your fortress, up on that peak over there.''

"That's it." Joe squinted. "But we're too far away to see what's up.''

Atlas stood, cradling the AK-47. "Let's get moving. We don't want to find ourselves pinned between the border patrol and these guys.''

Fifteen minutes later, they were about a hundred yards from the tower, lying behind a dense thicket of thorny scrub. Joe poked his head up to look around.

"You can see a little bit of the road, off to the right and beyond the tower. The doorway leading to the top of the tower is over on the left.''

Atlas raised his head and scanned the area. "Looks like there's a bunch grouped around that doorway. I think they're going to try storming the stairs.''

Joe said, "We'd better hurry up. I don't think Prynne and Phil can hold off much longer.''

The remaining members of the attack team were scattered in front of the tower, taking pot-shots at the top from their places of conceal-ment.

Atlas frowned. "You see the two over on the left of their line? The ones closest to the en-trance? We might just be able to take them without the others realizing it.''

The men in question shared the same cover, a large outcropping of stone. They were sepa-rated from the rest of the group.

Joe nodded. "If we can get their guns, we could charge the ones trying to storm the en-trance.''

They dropped on their bellies and crawled around the dense bushes, Atlas cradling the gun against his chest. To Joe, the crawl seemed endless—if any of the enemy just happened to look back for a second, matters could get very unpleasant very fast. But the men behind the rock kept their eyes on the tower.

When they came close enough to the two heavies, Atlas looked back at Joe, who nod-ded, scarcely breathing. Then he sprang for-ward, with Joe and Clea close behind.

Before the gunmen had time to move, Atlas was on them. He clubbed the first man on the back of the head with the automatic weapon. The other guy spun around, trying to get his gun into position, but Joe launched himself from a crouch to knock him down.

Joe grabbed his opponent, pulling him forward. Then he brought his right knee up into the man's jaw. The gunman's eyes went glassy, and he rolled onto his side. It was over in a few seconds.

None of the attackers had seen or heard a thing. Atlas removed the unconscious men's guns and ammunition. Joe took one AK-47 and passed the other to Clea, who took it reluctantly.

"It's set for automatic fire," instructed Joe. "Just squeeze the trigger to shoot. Remember: fire up in the air. This is just for effect, to scare those guys away from the stairway. Ready?"

Clea looked pale, but she nodded. "Even if I can't shoot, I can scream."

They grinned at each other.

Atlas slapped another magazine into his gun. "Right, here we go. Make a lot of noise. Joe, you sing out and make sure your friends don't mistake us for bad guys."

At a signal from Atlas, they sprang out from behind their shelter, guns pointed high, racing for the tower.

Five men knelt near the archway when the chaos exploded. They looked up to see three screaming maniacs practically on top of them, firing automatic weapons. Forgetting that they, too, had guns, they took to their heels in a total panic.

Joe Hardy fired his AK-47 and screamed as loud as he could: "Phil! Mr. P.! Hold your fire! We're coming in! Don't shoot!"

They dove into the archway as bullets from the attackers kicked up dust clouds and stone chips. But Phil and Prynne held their fire as Joe, Clea, and Atlas hurtled up the stairs and onto the tower roof, panting but unhurt.

Phil watched the three tumble in. "All right!" he said. "I'm glad you could drop by. Sorry I don't have time right now for socializing." He swung back and fired out at the gunmen below.

Atlas walked over to Morton Prynne, who sat with his back against a wall, covering the stairs. "Mr. Prynne, I presume? How's the leg?"

Prynne gave Atlas a thin smile. "Well, it isn't any better. But it isn't any worse either. Good to see you."

Atlas squatted down beside Prynne. "These kids of yours—I don't know where you picked them up—but they sure did a job."

Prynne's smile broadened. "Clea! Joe! Well

done! Now man a battle station. We still have to hold on until help arrives, but it's on the way."

"More company coming!" yelled Phil. "Looks like eight new arrivals down there!"

Joe, who had propped his gun on the wall near Phil, said, "Oh, yeah, we forgot to tell you—these guys have been on our tail all the way from the border."

Atlas joined the two at the wall and looked down, where the border patrol was now joining forces with the other group. "I make it to be about fifteen altogether." He frowned and looked at Joe. "Can't say that I like the odds."

Joe thought about their situation. "I don't know. There're more of them, but there're more of us, too, now."

"No," the agent said. "Having so many men down there gives them more firepower and mobility."

Atlas shook his head. "If they want me bad enough, they may just decide to take the casualties and try an all-out attack."

Chapter

17

THANKS TO FRANK'S WARNING, Spiros Stamos had two seconds to deal with the boulder. He stood on the brakes, bringing the car to a screeching stop. In the backseat Chet and the Gray Man were flung forward.

The boulder, with a thunderous roar, hit the road just ahead of the car, then tumbled down into the ravine. It had missed the front bumper by about a foot.

All the people in the car sat silent for a moment as they thought about the narrowness of their escape. Even the engine had stalled out.

Chet sat back in his seat with a soft "Wow!"

The Gray Man asked, "Is everyone okay?" Everyone seemed to be.

"You've got sharp reflexes, Mr. Stamos," Frank observed.

Andreas Stamos popped out from the bushes in which he had been hiding and dashed to the car. In his hand he held a small pocket mirror. "You saw my flashes?"

"They probably saved us from being squashed just then," said Frank. "Hop in, Andreas." Chet opened the back door and Andreas scrambled inside. His eyes were large with excitement, his words spilling out.

"I ran here and saw a car coming and hid because the car was full of strange men. Two of them climbed up—they were doing something to a big rock on the hill. When your car came they started pushing the rock, so I tried to signal you and—"

"And you succeeded and saved our lives," Stamos cut in. "Excellent work, son."

The Gray Man leaned across the back seat toward Andreas. "Did you see what happened to the men after they started the boulder downhill?"

Andreas nodded. "They ran that way," pointing toward where the secondary road branched off from the main one, "and then started down the hill."

"Then this is the turnoff we want to take to the fortress?" asked the Gray Man.

"It's about eight miles," Andreas said.

The Gray Man tapped Stamos on the shoulder. "They probably rejoined the others in their car, on their way to the fortress, or—"

"*Or*," cut in Frank, "they're planning a surprise for us ahead on the road."

"Well, whichever it is, we'd better get moving," the Gray Man responded.

Stamos brought the car's engine back to life, and they headed up the side road. It was narrower than the main route. Two cars meeting head-on would have had to pass each other very carefully.

They drove on, not too fast. Any curve could hide a trap set to spring on them. The minutes crawled by and each twist of the road became an adventure. The Gray Man reached down to the floor and began distributing guns. "Just in case. We don't want to be taken unprepared."

Frank examined his weapon, an American AR-14, which he had some experience with. He went back to watching the road. Was Joe back at the tower by now? Had he and Clea managed to bring the American agent back with them? Or—but there was no point in this kind of guesswork. He forced himself to concentrate on the matter in hand. Joe could take care of himself. Or, at any rate, he would have to, for the time being.

"Must be getting pretty close by now," Chet said. "Maybe those other guys just drove on up to the fortress."

"We are very near," Andreas agreed. "It will be up on a hill, to our left. You will go around a long curve, just ahead, and—"

Suddenly the rocky hills that bordered the road on the left broke off, forming a crevice, and out of that crevice a van appeared just behind them, greeting them with a hail of gunfire. Men leaned out of windows on both sides with automatic weapons blazing.

Stamos pressed down heavily on the gas pedal, trying to get a little distance between the two vehicles. Frank rolled down his window and aimed his gun back at the van. But in the bouncing, swaying car, it wasn't easy.

Chet peered back at the van from the back window. "Hey, Frank! You recognize the one riding shotgun?"

Frank knew that sharp face with the cold eyes, even when the eyes were squinting over the blazing barrel of an Uzi. "It's our old buddy, Theo. I figured we'd see him again before this was over." He fired a short burst, then corrected his aim.

"Go for the engine or the radiator!" the Gray Man shouted.

Frank grabbed at the door as the car took a sharp turn on two wheels. "I'll be lucky to hit anything, rocking and rolling like this!"

A series of metallic *thunks* and a shudder in the car showed that a gunman had stitched the trunk with bullets. Frank fired again, aiming lower.

The right front tire of the van blew out with a pop that could be heard in Salonika. The van lurched and swung wildly to the right, and then back the other way as the driver fought the wheel to keep the vehicle on the road. It fishtailed again with its tires squealing in protest, the van driver slamming on the brakes. Finally the van flipped over on its side and skidded.

Stamos brought the car to a halt, and Frank started to get out, but as he did, Theo pushed open the van door, firing at the car and forcing Frank back inside.

With Theo covering, another rider from the van managed to work his way out, carrying something in his arms. Both men sprinted away from the overturned van and away from the road. Frank realized that they were headed for the fortress.

Stamos grabbed Frank by the arm and pulled him into the car. "Shut the door! We must get up there fast."

Frank did as he was told, but as Stamos

gunned the car forward, he asked, "Why the big hurry?"

Stamos kept both eyes on the road. "Did you see what that fellow was carrying when he ran off toward the fort?"

"I couldn't tell what it was."

"Well, I've seen those things in action before. It was a mortar. They'll be able to lob shells right into the tower."

Stamos coaxed the car along the road while Theo and his friend ran cross-country.

"There it is!"

Andreas pointed to the fortress rising above the road.

Stamos stopped the car and the five passengers got out to look the situation over. They could hear firing, but from the road, there was no view of the action.

Suddenly the volume of fire increased sharply. "I'm going to take a look." Frank darted out from behind the car and worked his way uphill, toward the fort.

Moments later he raced back. Ducking down with the others, he drew a rough map in the dirt. "This is the fortress. And here is where they're setting up that mortar. They've got most of their firepower concentrated over *here,* well away from the mortar position, and they've opened up with heavy firing from that line.

"My guess is that the heavy firing is a diversion, to keep the defenders from noticing the mortar. Then they'll start lobbing shells into the tower. We'd better get that mortar out of commission fast."

The five moved hurriedly to the crest of the hill. Two men knelt by the mortar, stacking shells beside it.

"Where's Theo?" whispered Chet.

Frank whispered, "Maybe he's over where the shooting is coming from."

"We'll have to drive those men away from that field piece, that's the first priority," the Gray Man said.

They poured a hail of bullets over the heads of the two men, who immediately abandoned their position, dashing for cover.

The Gray Man called out, "Hold your fire!" The chattering of the guns stopped. "Frank, you and Chet stay here and keep anyone from reaching the mortar. If you can knock it out of action without exposing yourselves to any undue risk, do it. Spiros, you and Andreas come with me—we'll give those people doing all the shooting something else to worry about—a flank attack. Let's go."

While the Gray Man and the two Stamoses set off, Chet and Frank found cover. The mortar stood fifty feet away, with a pile of shells to one side and a few shells lying on the ground nearby.

"Maybe we could just rush out and grab that stovepipe," Chet suggested.

Frank shook his head. "Try it, and the crew will start sniping at you."

"Yeah, I guess. Boy, I feel like I haven't eaten in a week. You have any snacks, Frank?"

Shots rang out, *behind* Frank, and he actually heard the whine of a bullet zipping by him. He whipped around, and heard Chet cry out.

"Frank! It's Theo!"

The thin-faced thug had crept to within twenty feet of Frank and Chet, but his burst of fire had missed. Frank sent a short blast at the gunman, who ducked for the shelter of the thick, heavy branches of a dead tree.

Frank fired again, moving out to his left to get a better angle. Theo popped out from behind his tree trunk, aiming another volley at Frank, who dove headlong, hugging the ground as the shots passed harmlessly over his head. He heard a mocking laugh from behind the tree.

"You see, my young Yankee friend, I told you that we would meet once again."

Flat on his stomach, Frank raised his gun high, firing a long burst. Theo flinched back, but the bullets went over his head. He stepped round the tree, his face an ugly mask of triumph as he leveled his Uzi at Frank. "I want you dead, Yankee."

Then the massive tree branch that Frank's shooting had torn loose from the trunk dropped on Theo's head. Frank smiled as Theo folded into an unconscious heap. "You're lucky I wanted *you* alive," he said.

He dragged Theo over to the tree and tied him so that his arms circled the trunk. Then he hurried back to Chet, who said, "I thought he had you there for a second."

"Good thing that tree was dead, or I don't know if that trick would've worked. Now, about that mortar . . . I wonder if we could set off one of those loose shells over there by shooting it."

"Want to try?"

"If it goes up, it'll probably take those other shells with it, so let's back off."

They moved away to some rocks that stood forty yards from the mortar. Frank tapped Chet on the shoulder. "If this works, don't stand there admiring the explosion. Hit the dirt."

They began firing short bursts at the shells. The first few did nothing but raise dust clouds. Then there was a loud *crack!* and a fiery flash, followed almost immediately by a really thunderous roar.

Frank and Chet dove behind their shelter

with the first explosion. But they felt the shockwave and the heat from the big blast as the entire stack of shells went up. A scattering of debris fell around them. They waited a bit, and then slowly raised themselves up for a look.

The mortar lay some distance from where it had been, a twisted and bent metal tube. There was a shallow crater where the shells had been.

"Awesome!" Chet's eyes were wide.

Frank's ears were ringing. "Come on," he said to Chet. "Let's give the others a hand. We're not out of the woods yet."

They found Spiros and Andreas Stamos with the Gray Man exchanging fire with a group of enemy gunmen. The Gray Man twisted around to give Frank a startled glance.

"Five or six men have us pinned in place here, and I think most of the rest are trying a last-ditch attack on the tower."

The intensity of gunfire abruptly rose, coming from the vicinity of the entryway leading to the tower, and from the top of the tower itself.

"This could be it," the Gray Man muttered.

Spiros Stamos called out from his position, "What can we do?"

Frank thought of his brother, up there facing an all-out assault. "We've got to do something!"

The Gray Man reached out and gripped Frank by the shoulder. "Listen to me. Trying to get over to them now would be suicidal. They have us pinned down here. We wouldn't—"

"Hey!" Chet piped up. "Listen a second!"

Frank listened, frowning. "I can't hear— Wait a minute! It sounds like—a car."

A khaki-colored troop carrier with the Greek flag painted on its door pulled up. Troops hopped out, forming up in ranks.

Chet jumped up. "Look! The attackers are splitting!"

The men who'd been massing to attack the tower were now retreating in haste, into the hills and back to the Yugoslav border. The wounded were being hauled along by their comrades.

"Why don't you go and round them up?" Chet demanded.

"We have what we want—it's much better to pretend all this never happened." The Gray Man shot a look of warning at Frank and Chet.

"I hope we can count on you never to talk about this, to anyone, under any circumstances whatever. You went to Greece, looked at ruins and the countryside, made a little side trip, and you went home. Period."

"What about Peter being kidnapped?" asked

Frank. "The students all were there when that went down."

"They've been told that it was all a misunderstanding. Peter went home with some relatives and didn't tell us in advance. And the attack at the restaurant had nothing whatever to do with us. Clear?"

"Clear," said Chet with regret in his voice.

"Frank! Hey, Frank!" Joe Hardy walked toward them, supporting Morton Prynne on one side while Atlas supported the other. "I never thought I'd be so happy to see you again!"

Andreas Stamos dashed ahead and hugged Clea. Peter and Spiros ran over, too, and the four Stamoses met in a big embrace. Atlas and the Gray Man started to move away with them, but Frank stopped the Network agent.

"Just about a hundred yards back that way, you'll find a guy tied to a tree," he said. "His name is Theo, and he's the head bad guy."

"Nicholas Kaliotis will tell us all we need to put Theo away," said Spiros Stamos. He shook hands with Frank and Joe in turn and said, "Thank you, both. I cannot say how grateful I am."

Stamos turned to the Gray Man. "These young men are valuable assets. Perhaps one day you might formalize their position."

The Gray Man coughed. "Ah, yes, I must admit that they did quite well, considering—"

"That we're only amateurs," said Frank and Joe in chorus.

"Frank. Joe." It was Morton Prynne, now supported by two Greek soldiers in fatigues. "You're a couple of very remarkable young men. And you have some remarkable friends."

Joe stepped forward. "And you're a tough dude, Mr. P. Take care of that leg, now."

"Joe," said Clea softly, coming toward him. Joe smiled and stuck out his hand.

Clea ignored the hand, reached up, and kissed him softly on the cheek.

"I'll try not to think so badly of Americans," she said, smiling. "Or, at least, I will always think *very* well of one young American man."

Joe looked into those deep, dark eyes. "Clea, you're something else. There's no one I'd trust more in a tight spot, male *or* female."

Frank pulled Joe to one side. "Can I believe my ears? Or am I hallucinating?"

Joe glared at Frank. "Hey, give me a break! There's an exception to every rule, and she happens to be it."

Frank nodded, pretending to consider Joe's statement very carefully. "Well, then, can I tell our friends back in Bayport that you now realize that there are women who can stand up

148

to men in physical endurance and clutch situations?"

Joe said, "That can only be revealed on a need-to-know basis." He grinned. "And I hope *that* is something no one will *ever* need to know!"

Frank and Joe's next case:

The Hardys fly to Alaska to trace Scott Sanders, who's supposed to be working on a top-secret project for a mining firm. When company officials claim they've never heard of Scott, the Hardys grow suspicious. They find that some company managers have been selling jobs on the big oil pipeline.

But before the brother detectives can dig deeper, they're kidnapped and forced to bail out over the Arctic wilderness. Stranded, Frank and Joe face their toughest test—fighting hunger, grizzly bears, and bullets to survive—while at trail's end a group called the Assassins waits to give them their final exam . . . in *Trouble in the Pipeline,* Case #26 in The Hardy Boys Casefiles™.

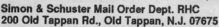